DESCENDANT

A.L. KNORR

MARTHA CARR

DESCENDANT

The Kacy Chronicles Book 1
By A.L. Knorr and Martha Carr

From A.L. Knorr

For anyone who ever wished they could fly.

From Martha

To everyone who still believes in magic and all the possibilities that holds.
To all the readers who make this entire ride so much fun.
And to all the dreamers just like me who create wonder, big and small, every day.

DESCENDANT TEAM

JIT BETA READERS

Alex Wilson
James Caplan
Joshua Ahles
Keith Verret
Kelly ODonnell
Kimberly Boyer
Micky Cocker
Paul Westman
Peter Manis
Nicola Aquino

If we missed anyone, please let us know!

A part of
The Revelations of Oriceran Universe
Written and Created
by Michael Anderle & Martha Carr

The Oriceran Universe
(and what happens within / characters / situations / worlds) are
Copyright (c) 2017 by Martha Carr and LMPBN Publishing.

DESCENDANT (this book) is a work of fiction.

All of the characters, organizations, and events portrayed in this novel are either products of the author's imagination or are used fictitiously. Sometimes both.

This book Copyright © 2017 A.L. Knorr and Martha Carr

Cover Design by Damonza

Cover copyright © LMBPN Publishing

LMBPN Publishing supports the right to free expression and the value of copyright. The purpose of copyright is to encourage writers and artists to produce the creative works that enrich our culture.

The distribution of this book without permission is a theft of the author's intellectual property. If you would like permission to use material from the book (other than for review purposes), please contact info@kurtherianbooks.com. Thank you for your support of the author's rights.

LMBPN Publishing

PMB 196, 2540 South Maryland Pkwy

Las Vegas, NV 89109

First US edition, September 2017

Version 1.13 January 2018

The Oriceran Universe (and what happens within / characters / situations / worlds) are Copyright (c) 2017 by Martha Carr and LMBPN Publishing.

❦ Created with Vellum

PROLOGUE

Two hundred eighty years before Virginia became a Commonwealth, a pair of tiny gnomish hands dug into the rich soil of what would one day become plantation land outside of Richmond.

Under the cover of darkness, under a sky speckled with stars, a silent gnome pressed the seedling of an oak into its forever home in the earth. Gingerly, he held the stem upright and lovingly snugged the earth around it.

He uttered an enchantment over the sprout and its tender leaves glowed momentarily. The gnome drew symbols into the air and a hole slid open there – the veil between the worlds temporarily rent. The passage was just large enough to accommodate him. He squeezed through and disappeared, leaving the seedling alone. The wind blew through its unremarkable leaves and branches; now one of thousands, indistinguishable from the rest.

The oak grew, reaching its mighty branches to the sky in a slow relentless march – a humble force of nature, its secrets locked away. A silent giant and sentinel of the forest, it would weather storms and wars, slavery and prosperity. Presidents and movie stars waxed and waned and still it grew.

Still it waited.

CHAPTER 1

Jordan steered her BMW convertible onto the narrow paved road, the last turn before she reached the driveway of the Kacy plantation, her family's summer home in Hanover County, Virginia, the tomato capital of the South.

Branches of towering oaks criss-crossed over the narrow lane, making a welcoming arch over the home stretch. Cicadas buzzed and frogs belted tunes from the swamps on either side of the road. They were feeling the change in the energy floating through the air—chirping and squawking as though in anticipation of something. Lines of sunlight flashed over the car through gaps in the canopy overhead, stealing focus from the sounds in the background.

Jordan inhaled deeply in the humid air and pushed her sunglasses back into her blonde hair. The stress of her exams for her Bachelor's in linguistics finally began to melt away. She was free for the summer. Free to work in the garden, hang out with her father, go horseback riding and maybe arrange a long hike in the Appalachians with her friends.

Jordan's eyes dropped to the clock on her console. Her dad should be waiting for her by the time she arrived.

As though on cue, her phone chirped from its holder. Allan Kacy, a state senator to most, "Dad" to Jordan. She pressed the 'answer' button on her steering wheel.

"Hey, Dad." She was unable to keep the grin out of her voice. "I'm less than five minutes away."

"Hi, Jordy," came Allan's throaty bass through her car's speakers. "I'm running behind. Got caught up with a lobbyist this afternoon and I'm still stuck on an issue with her."

"Daaaaaaaad."

"I know, I know. I'm almost done, I promise. I'll be hitting the road shortly. Can't wait to see you."

Jordan slowed the convertible as she approached their driveway and steered the car up to their aluminum mailbox. She opened the box and caught a week's worth of flyers and newspapers as they tumbled out. "Want me to start a fire?" she asked him. She tossed the load of mail onto the passenger's seat and her eye caught on a white delivery notice. She picked it up and scanned it.

"It's June, baby. Is that really necessary?"

"No, it isn't. But you know how cozy it makes the place. Hey, there's a delivery for you at the post office. Did you order something?"

The phone went silent.

"Dad?"

"Um…"

Jordan laughed. "What is it this time? A helmet from the Boer War, or a pair of boots worn by General Marshall?" Allan was a collector of war memorabilia. There was an entire upstairs room at the plantation dedicated to his obsession. If you were brave enough to quiz Allan on either WWI or WWII trivia, you'd better be prepared to settle in for a long night.

"Wait till you see it," Allan said and his voice sounded totally different. Younger. Full of life. "It's a beauty. I was lucky to find it, actually."

"Sounds expensive," Jordan said. "You only say that when you've spent more than a grand." Jordan hit the remote fastened to her sun visor and the wrought-iron gates began their slow, squeaky separation. She eased the convertible through the narrow entrance and down the long, potholed driveway. "Still don't get why you didn't become a history prof, Dad."

"There's no money in teaching history," Allan scoffed.

"Well, not our kind of money," said Jordan as she pulled up in front of their towering heritage home. "But you might have been happier."

"I'm not unhappy, Jordy. But I do have to go. I'll catch up to you soon, okay?"

"Kay, Dad. See you in a bit." Jordan hung up and frowned. Allan wasn't happy, actually; he just didn't want to admit it to his daughter. Going into politics had been his father's decision, not his own.

She took her earpiece out, threw it into her bag, grabbed the stack of mail and got out of the convertible. Taking the front steps two at a time, Jordan paused to sniff the wisteria that had a stranglehold on the fat marble columns gracing their front porch. She used her key to let herself in through the wide double doors. She crossed the foyer, purposefully stepping on the squeaky floorboard and smiled at the familiar sound. She tossed the mail on the huge round table in the center of the room. Fresh peonies —multi-colored and fragrant–stood in a large crystal vase in the middle of the table. Jordan leaned over the table to take a whiff. Cal, their groundskeeper, had probably left shortly before she'd arrived. He always set out some impressive bouquet whenever Jordan and Allan were coming to the house. He could do anything with plants and kept the Kacy plantation manicured all by himself. It was a full-time job.

Jordan slipped into the small bathroom that was tucked under the wide, curved staircase and took out her contacts. Her eyes were instantly grateful for the fresh air. Her reflection in the small mirror went blurry and Jordan fumbled in her bag for her glasses case. The world came back into focus as she put on her trendy specs with the black frames. It was impossible for her to navigate the world without either them or her contacts.

She went through the broad archway into the sitting room—a massive space filled with clusters of antique furniture and a big fireplace. An antique crank gramophone sat on a table under a window, its brass parts gleaming. Jordan's mother had loved antiques and, according to Allan, the gramophone had been one of her favorite pieces.

Jordan heard the fire crackling before she saw it or felt its heat.

"You beauty, Cal," she said to the elderly fellow who was still down on one knee in front of the fire, rearranging the logs with a poker. Cal was a small, wiry man with dark brown eyes and deep laugh lines. He'd been keeping the grounds for the Kacy family since Jordan was in diapers and knew that she loved to have a fire in the parlor in the evenings.

He looked up and winked. "Miss Kacy," he nodded. "How did your exams go?"

"Really well; thanks, Cal. It's nice to find you still here. How's the wife?"

His phone dinged from the front bib of his denim coveralls. "Impatient," he chuckled. "I'll be heading out now. Just didn't want to leave the fire unattended." He got to his feet stiffly, and scratched his forehead. "Allan working late?"

"Seems so," said Jordan, coming to stand in front of the fire. "He'll be along soon. You go home. Have a good weekend." She reached out and squeezed his arm. "Thanks for the fire."

He touched a finger to the brim of his cap. "Welcome. Have a good time with your pa."

Jordan stood watching the flames and chewing her lip for a

while after Cal left. Her eyes drifted to the mantel, where a collection of family photographs stood, becoming artifacts of history. Her mother's face smiled down from the cluster of images, impossible to ignore with its otherworldly beauty: accepting a bouquet after winning the Miss Virginia pageant, in a debutante dress, bare-shouldered and with an arm looped through the elbow of Jordan's grandfather, Declin Richard Kacy. Tantalizing in a strapless cream gown with dusty-pink tea-roses at the nape of her neck, Jaclyn had the kind of face and figure only found in magazines and on movie screens. A tall and leggy brown-eyed blonde, with high cheekbones and a pouty mouth, she had won several pageants, modelling contracts and even the role of spokesperson for an environmentally-friendly beauty brand. When Jaclyn, the sweetheart of Richmond, met Allan Kacy at a ribbon-cutting ceremony for a new children's hospital, they seemed destined for a happy ending and a house full of exquisitely beautiful children, living along stately River Road—or at least nestled somewhere in the West End.

Jordan selected one of the photographs and took it down—the black and white portrait of her mother in the antique silver frame. She gazed into the dark brown doe-eyes and frowned. "What happened to you, Mom?" she whispered. It was the defining question of Jordan's youth.

Jaclyn had disappeared when Jordan was not yet three and Jordan no longer knew if the faint memories she had of her mother were real or figments of her imagination. A long-familiar pang struck Jordan in the heart and her throat closed up, more with sadness for her father than for herself. But still she wondered, what kind of woman would she have been if she had been raised with the help of her mother's hand? Jaclyn had been beloved. Allan had only ever spoken of her wit, her wisdom and her sweetness.

There had been no note, suicide or otherwise. There had been no signs of a struggle and no body had ever been found. Jaclyn's

Porsche had still been parked in the garage, the engine cool. Her bike still hung on the rack along with Jordan's and Allan's. Her luggage was stowed in the attic; all of her clothing was still hanging and folded in her closets. The only indication that Jaclyn was gone had been the open back door. The old plantation property had miles of forests and farmland to the west and south, swampland to the east and the interstate to the north. How far could she have gone when leaving the house on foot? The property's old well was covered with a concrete slab and the large pond at the rear of their yard had been dragged three times over.

According to Allan and the investigator leading the missing persons case, it seemed as though Jaclyn had literally disappeared without a trace. The only factor the investigators had to go on was that Jaclyn was still struggling with fairly serious postpartum depression.

So where did that leave the Kacy family?

"Nowhere, that's where," Jordan muttered, putting the photograph back on the mantel.

CHAPTER 2

Sol heard the harpy before he saw it. The whistling, half-scream half-roar couldn't be mistaken for anything else. Miles of wilderness coastline flew by underneath him, unguarded and unprotected. This was the most dangerous stretch between Rodania and Maticaw; still, it was rare to see harpies this far south. Sol cursed under his breath as another scream rent the air. Even the sound of the crashing waves breaking against the rocks below couldn't drown out that wretched cry.

Sol's enormous tawny wings pumped with slow, powerful strokes, catching an updraft and taking him higher. Being an Arpak, a winged human, meant that the sky should be his territory. Harpies used to be a non-issue, but they were becoming a menace and growing bolder by the day.

He craned his neck, but couldn't see the harpy through the cloud cover. He climbed higher in search of the top of the stratocumulus. Fog swirled around him in little cyclones as he powered his way up, his wings pumping.

Breaking through the cloud cover, he leveled out and shut the nictitating membranes over his eyes. Nothing but thick gray fluff could be seen behind him, but ahead of him it thinned and he could make out a line of green below. The cliffs were coming to an end and the forest was growing thick. Sol smiled grimly. Harpies and forests didn't mix well. The woods represented his only opportunity to shake them off. He didn't relish the thought of one-on-one aerial combat with a harpy—no matter how many tricks he'd learned at the academy.

As the clouds thinned, he tucked his wings behind him and angled downward, his body now a bullet streaking toward the earth. As he dropped below the cloud, another hair-raising screech sounded from behind him. Too close. Looking back, he saw a dark shape, broad and powerful; leathery, dragon-like wings driving the beast forward like the pistons of some great machine. Sol faced front and streaked downward before leveling out over the treetops.

Another glance back had his heart in his mouth.

There are two of them, now? And they were gaining, fast. He could make out the wrinkled skin of their foreheads and their flat red eyes. Sol didn't have time to process how strange it was to see two harpies hunting together. Everything he'd learned, everything he knew up until this point, identified them as solitary beasts.

Sol swallowed as their external teeth came into focus. It was far too detailed a visual for his comfort. He skimmed over the treetops with hard, powerful strokes, watching for a break in the canopy. Harpies were larger and stronger than Arpaks, but they weren't nearly as nimble. The odds that they'd follow him into the trees were low, he hoped.

The throaty screech behind him, closer yet, made his decision for him. At the next break in the canopy, he dove. Holding his breath, Sol broke through the treetops and dropped face-first with his forearms up in front of him. This kind of maneuver through a tight space was dangerous for an Arpak, even in a forest of giant dreesha—trees so big and tall, there was a whole new layer of atmosphere underneath them.

Branches scratched and clawed at Sol's arms and leather clothing, as he broke through at a speed he would never attempt if it weren't a life-or-death situation. Taking a glancing blow off a thick dreesha limb, Sol lost a bit of speed and wobbled before righting himself below the canopy. He picked up speed again and worked to maintain his height in the strip of atmosphere between the dreesha canopy and the second canopy of trees below him. Light filtered through the trees in soft pillars, flashing in Sol's eyes as he flew.

The sound of snapping and breaking branches made Sol take a sharp breath.

They're following me?

Sol gritted his teeth as both harpies let off simultaneous screams. He heard the cracking of breaking limbs and then the sound of something heavy landing in the canopy below and behind him. He glanced down to see a thick dreesha limb fall and crash through the more fragile bottom canopy, leaving a gaping hole. Squawking birds flew up from the trees, scolding the harpies for disrupting them.

Sol's right hand went down to his blade and his left hand reached back over his shoulder to grasp a short spear from his quiver.

If I am going to have to fight...

Sol didn't finish the thought as he saw a break in the canopy beneath him. Surely they wouldn't follow him down even further; they couldn't maneuver at all through a forest of the much smaller oaks. Encouraged by the idea, Sol dove towards the break.

Realizing their prey was going to evade them, the harpies screamed a grating, eardrum-destroying cry. The sound of their leathery wings bellowing against the air spurred Sol on. He didn't dare look back, but every hair on his body stood at attention, anticipating a rake of claws across his legs at any moment. One swipe of those nasty talons and he was very likely finished–if the wounds didn't kill him, the infection would.

Pinning his wings back and praying for a safe break through the canopy, he braced himself. Yellow sparks and flashes of light went off in his vision. Before Sol had time to realize what he was seeing, he was through the break. His sight went black and the sounds of a thousand voices and crackling lightning filled his ears. There was a bone-breaking, tooth-jarring impact and Sol knew no more.

CHAPTER 3

"I was beginning to get worried," said Jordan from the front steps as Allan got out of his Land Rover. His ginger hair was ruffled from driving with the windows down and his glasses were dusty. Allan was a tall, slight man with a narrow face and generous lips. He was pale, freckled and handsome in his way. Fine lines bracketed his mouth and Jordan frowned at the dark smudges under his eyes. "Tough week?" She crossed the gravel and helped her dad bring his small suitcase, laptop bag and briefcase inside the manor.

"Very," Allan sighed. He set down his bag and pulled his daughter in for a hug. "I'm destroyed. Is there any bourbon left?" He released Jordan, reached into his suit coat pockets and dumped a handful of paper money, change and receipts onto the foyer table.

"Well I sure don't drink the stuff," Jordan shuddered. "That bad, huh? You going to numb yourself with alcohol until the pain of politics goes away?"

Allan laughed. "I don't think there's enough alcohol in the world to accomplish that monumental task." They passed into the parlor. "You did light the fire, after all," Allan observed as he collapsed onto the sofa in front of the flames, toeing off his dress shoes and stretching his legs out in front of him. "You're such an amphibian. Always with the cold toes, just like your mother." Jordan was familiar with the stories of Jaclyn freezing Allan in bed with her cold feet.

"Cal lit it," Jordan said as she crossed to the sideboard. "He was here when I arrived."

"Good ol' Cal," Allan mused fondly.

A wide variety of hard liquor was displayed on the antique wooden sideboard and backed by a mirror, making the selection look twice as bountiful. Jordan removed the lid from the bourbon decanter and poured a drink. Her dad took it neat; no water, no ice, no nothing but nose-singeing, throat-closing alcohol. He swore it went down smooth. Jordan held the bourbon away from her nose so she didn't have to smell it and delivered it to her dad.

"How did your exams go?" Allan asked her as she plopped down beside him and kicked off her sneakers.

"Aced them," she sang. Jordan came from a long line of overachievers, which she fit right into like a set of those multi-colored Russian dolls.

"Atta girl. Any thoughts on where you want to do your Masters? Maybe VCU, so you can stay close to home?"

Jordan shrugged. Allan always brought the conversation to the future and Jordan was usually prepared, but this time, she didn't have any firm answers. "I was thinking Europe, maybe Spain?"

Allan took off his glasses and rubbed the bridge of his nose. "Why? It's a cutting-edge industry and America is the tip of the sword."

"I don't know, Dad. How about we just chill out and enjoy the weekend? You want to go to the stables tomorrow? Go for a ride?"

"Maybe Sunday," Allan replied. He waggled his eyebrows at

Jordan. "I'm gonna pick up my new toy. You want to help me set it up?"

"What is it?"

Allan leaned back and slid down into the soft cushions. "I wouldn't want to spoil the surprise," he said with a grin that Jordan was sure hadn't changed since he was a little boy.

"I won't be tricked into lining up four thousand teensy toy soldiers like last time," Jordan tilted her head down and gave him a look.

Allan bellowed and slapped his knee. "That was a good one."

"If Mom had been here, she would have skinned you for making me do that," Jordan laughed.

Allan's smile faltered. His hazel eyes flicked to the photographs on the mantel and then back down to the fire.

"Her birthday is next week," Jordan said. "You want to go visit the grave?"

The frown that crossed Allan's brow was there and gone so fast, Jordan wondered if she'd imagined it. Allan took a breath and looked over at his daughter, at her beautiful teal eyes—the shape of Jaclyn's—and her thick lashes.

"Why don't we make that an every-five-years event instead of an annual one, Jordy?"

Jordan blinked and the corners of her mouth turned down. "Because that's how she would be slowly forgotten," she said quietly. "Is that what you would want, if it were you?"

"Yes," Allan said immediately. "I would want my loved ones to move on, not hang on to the dead."

"We don't know for sure that she's dead." Jordan began the debate that was as old as her ability to have an adult conversation with her father.

"She's dead, darling." Allan pinned Jordan with a look. It was compassionate, but resolute. "And she wouldn't want you to go on holding out hope for the impossible."

"No body, no proof," Jordan replied. "You had the headstone

erected in Hollywood Cemetery for Grandma and Grandpa so they could have some closure before they died, but it's still just a stone atop an empty plot of earth."

Allan sighed and, with one hand, rubbed his eyes underneath the frames of his glasses. He dropped his head back on the top of the sofa and rested his bourbon glass on the arm of the couch. "I don't think it's healthy, Jordan."

"You didn't raise me to give up," said Jordan, stoutly.

"I didn't raise you to waste your youth pining for a dead woman, either." Allan spoke so sharply it was almost a bark.

Jordan tensed, stung. She had never heard her father refer to her mother as a 'dead woman' before. It was so impersonal, so cold. "Dad…"

Allan sat up and turned to her, regret etched into his features. He put a warm palm on the back of her hand. "I'm sorry. You know I loved your mother more than I loved anyone. There just comes a time when you have to move on. You've been so loyal, so devoted to her; to a fault, Jordan." Allan sliced a hand through the air. "It's time to pack up all that memorabilia you have in your room," he gestured to the photos on the mantel, "and everywhere else."

Jordan's eyes widened.

Allan's voice softened at the look of horror on his daughter's face. "I'm not saying to forget entirely; I would never tell you to do that. Just…" he gestured toward the line of frames holding various images of Jaclyn, "pick one and let that be it. This place feels like a shrine."

Allan got up and went to stand in front of the fireplace. His hand was up on the mantel, but his eyes looked down into the dwindling fire.

"I'm going to turn in for the night," Jordan said.

"Jordy—" Allan said, turning. "Don't go to bed mad."

"I'm not mad, Dad. Just tired," Jordan said. She got up and went to kiss Allan's cheek. "Have a good sleep."

Allan kissed her cheek in return and wondered if he'd spoken too soon. He watched his daughter leave the parlor and he set his jaw. *No, it isn't too soon. My daughter is an adult now. Pining is unhealthy. It would be better for her not to be reminded of her mother every time she was in this house, every time she looked up.*

Allan's hazel eyes went to the image of Jaclyn in her debutante dress. Her painfully beautiful face smiled down at him. That smile used to warm him to his toes, but now it taunted him. He set his bourbon down on the mantel and began to take the pictures off the wooden shelf. The one that showed her holding flowers and standing next to her father in his black tails—their wedding photograph. The casual shot of her, taken on the tree-swing hanging from the old oak in the back yard. One by one, he took them down and tucked them into the cupboard under the bookshelf.

By the time Allan doused the flames and went to bed, there was only one shot of Jaclyn left in the room. It was a small, oval portrait, hidden among a collection of them hanging on the wall behind the grand piano. Now hers was just one picture among many.

CHAPTER 4

The next morning, only five minutes after her dad had left, the sound of gravel popping under car tires drew Jordan to the window. She squinted at the silver Rav4 with the rental plate that came to a stop in front of the manor. The silhouette of long hair didn't help Jordan identify the driver through the windshield, but when the door popped open and a dark-haired woman with an olive complexion got out, Jordan gasped.

Jordan rushed through the parlor and the foyer to open the front door and greet her nanny of thirteen years. Throwing the doors open wide, she cried, "Maria!"

Maria's lined, gunmetal-gray eyes misted over and her face lit up. "Bambina, look what a beautiful woman you've become." She opened her arms wide.

Jordan melted against the bosom of the woman who'd been the only mother she'd ever known. "We haven't seen you in years," Jordan said, pulling back to look at Maria's face. The added lines and gray hairs couldn't diminish Maria's matronly beauty. "Come in, come in. What are you doing here?"

"I'm sorry I didn't warn you I was coming. Sort of a last-second decision," Maria said, as they passed into the house.

Jordan thought Maria's accent seemed stronger than usual. *Perhaps she's been spending more time in Belize with her extended family.* "Is your father home?" Maria asked. Her gray eyes searched the foyer and she peeked into the parlor.

Jordan noticed how Maria's brows drew together. *Is that fear in her eyes?* Jordan dismissed it. Maria had no reason to fear Allan; the two of them were thick as thieves while Jordan was growing up. A time or two, she'd even suspected they cared far more for each other than they let on; she had even daydreamed that one day Maria would become her mother by marrying Allan. But it never came to be.

"Not at the moment, he's gone to the post office to pick up a package. Come in. I have some of that lavender iced tea that you love."

Maria looked relieved. "No, thank you, sweetheart. I'm really just passing through on my way to the airport. I can't stay." Her eyes flashed to the driveway through the front window.

"Oh, that's a shame," Jordan said, surprised. "Where are you going? Back to Belize for a visit?"

Maria ignored the question and set her cloth purse on the foyer table and then rifled through it. "I just wanted to drop something off—something that I thought you should have." She withdrew a small white box tied with a blue satin ribbon.

Jordan's eyebrows shot up. "You got me a present?" Her eyes went to the white box; curious as to what kind of gift a nanny of years past would give a girl who had everything. She took the box from Maria and pulled her into another hug. "You're so sweet." She grasped the end of the blue ribbon.

Maria put a hand on top of Jordan's, staying her fingers. "Don't open it now," she said, her cheeks coloring. "Wait till I'm gone." Her eyes misted up again and she brushed them away with the side of her hand.

"Hey," Jordan said, putting a hand on Maria's shoulder. "What's going on?"

Maria smiled at her through weepy eyes. "I'm moving back to Belize."

"You're moving? Like, for good?"

"Yes, my family needs me." She squeezed Jordan's shoulders. "I'm sorry this is such an abrupt goodbye." She began to move toward the door. "I'm afraid I didn't plan very well."

"Wait." Jordan trailed after her, anxiety twisting in her gut. "Don't you want to say goodbye to Dad?"

Maria stepped out onto the driveway. She looked up at Jordan as she pulled the car's door open. Jordan stopped abruptly at the flash of grief in her nanny's eyes. It was only there for a moment, but it was enough to set Jordan's heart pounding.

"I can't, dear. I'm already late." Maria's voice broke and she cleared her throat.

"Maria-" Jordan began. "Is it your family? Is someone sick?"

"Take care of each other," Maria said. She slipped into the driver's side and closed the door.

Jordan walked to the driver's side window. "Wait!"

What was with her loved ones these days? First her dad seemed to want to skip over the visit to her mother's gravesite and now her nanny, not seen in years, couldn't seem to get off their property fast enough. Jordan felt disappointment clutch at her belly.

Maria kissed her fingers, put her palm flat against the glass and mouthed, "Goodbye." A tear slipped from her eye and she wiped her cheek as the car pulled away.

Jordan watched the vehicle circle the drive and then disappear beneath the canopy of oaks. She stood there for several minutes after the vehicle had gone, her heart heavy and her mind bemused. She went back inside, the floorboards squeaking as she approached the foyer table and picked up the small white box. Pulling the ribbon off and lifting the lid revealed an antique silver locket and chain, nestled in cotton. She picked it up and marvelled at the cold weight of it. The locket had delicate scrollwork around the outside and a strange flourish in the center; a symbol of some kind. She turned it over and saw the repeated pattern on the back. Her thumb found the small silver clasp and the locket snapped open.

Jordan gasped and adjusted her glasses. Stepping through the open front door, she held the locket in a beam of morning sunlight. Her hand flew to her mouth. Inside the locket was a hand-painted portrait of her mother. Jaclyn's face was relaxed in a closed-mouth smile; her brown eyes wide open and focused slightly upward. Her brunette hair was pulled half-back and it cascaded down behind her ears and over her collarbone. The painting was a perfect likeness; just the hairstyle seemed strange, like she had dressed for a starring role in a movie.

Jordan grabbed her purse off the table and fumbled inside it for her phone. Holding the locket open in one hand, she turned on her phone with the other and gave it a verbal command. "Call Maria," she ordered. "Turn on speakerphone." The phone dialed and two long dashes sounded.

"The number you are calling is no longer in service," answered the electronic voice.

"What?" Jordan said aloud with surprise. "Hang up," she commanded. She scrolled through her contacts and checked the number she had entered for Maria. She frowned. The digits seemed right, but she hadn't called Maria in a long time. *Maybe she's changed her number? But then, why not give me the new number before she left?* Maria didn't use email, so phoning was the only way to get a hold of her. Jordan didn't even have an address for her in Belize. "Dial Maria," Jordan said again and waited.

"The number you are calling is no longer in service," repeated the voice.

Jordan hung up the phone and let out a frustrated breath. *Where did Maria get the locket? Why does it have a portrait of my mother inside it and how long has Maria had it?* Questions elbowed one another in Jordan's mind. The locket had obviously belonged to her mother first, so how had it come to be in Maria's possession?

Time slipped by as Jordan stared at her mother's image, chewing her lip and mentally stewing. When the sound of Allan's Land Rover coming up the driveway reached her ears, Jordan headed out to meet him. *Maybe he'll know something about the locket.*

CHAPTER 5

"Jordan!" Allan called as he got out of the Land Rover. "Would you mind grabbing that dolly from the basement and helping your old dad?" He was practically dancing in place with excitement.

Jordan halted and headed back into the house, tossing a question over her shoulder. "What did you buy, a Panzer?"

Allan let out a contagious giggle and Jordan couldn't help but laugh.

"You'll see," he teased.

"Where is the dolly?"

"In that little closet next to the potato cellar." His brows drew together for a moment as a thought occurred. "Think you'll need help carrying it?"

Jordan rolled her eyes. She climbed and ran regularly and had even won her division in the Richmond Marathon, beating the tall hill at the end, known as 'Lee's Revenge,' that had stopped many a runner from finishing. And yet, somehow, her father still saw her as a little girl who would need a man to open the pickle jar for her. "I'll be right there."

She made her way down into the cool, dusty bowels of the

manor. The dolly was just where Allan had said it would be. She hiked back upstairs with the metal contraption, swung open the front doors and pushed the dolly through.

Allan had the back of the Land Rover open and a wooden crate was sitting on the tailgate.

"Sweet mother of crap, Dad. That box is huge. What did you buy?"

Allan grinned. "Help me get it on the dolly and up the stairs."

The two of them got the crate balanced on the metal platform and Allan wheeled it backwards across the gravel to the steps, where Jordan pushed it from underneath to get it up the stairs.

As they rolled the dolly and its burden across the foyer, the floorboard squeaked under Allan's foot.

"I really need to fix that board," he grunted.

"Don't you dare," replied Jordan. "I love that board. I used to listen for it at night when I was a little girl. When I heard the squeak, I knew you were home."

Allan smiled as they backed the dolly wheels up to the next set of steps. "As you wish."

With a rhythm of pulling and lifting, they got the wooden box up the grand staircase and down the hall to Allan's favorite room - his war room.

This room was the man cave to end all man caves, made even better by the two dormers and window seats that overlooked the backyard. A low bookshelf crammed with a multitude of books about WWI and WWII lined the back wall. Model ships, tanks and planes, which Allan had lovingly built himself, graced the bookshelf's top. Wooden shelves along the other walls artfully displayed boots, helmets, weapons, journals, old maps, goggles, gas masks and every other imaginable thing one would expect to see in a war museum.

In the back corner was a model landscape that Allan used to recreate battles while reading the details from a memoir or history book. Allan sometimes invited Cal up to play–since Cal was fond of history too—and the two of them would debate, sometimes loudly, over the merits of Patton's battle strategy, or how WWII was really won.

They laid the crate down on the floor and Allan took a kerchief out of his back pocket to mop his face. "You're not even sweating," he said to his daughter.

Jordan grabbed the small pry-bar from her father's desk and handed it to him. "I work out. You should try it sometime."

Allan stuck his tongue out and Jordan laughed. "If only your constituents could see you now."

Nothing turned Allan into a child like adding an item to his collection. Allan took the bar and worked the crate lid off, the nails protesting as they came loose from the wood. Cornstarch peanuts and styrofoam blocks hid everything that was inside except for a rounded piece of tarnished metal. Allan pulled at the styrofoam and brushed away the peanuts, letting them fly out of the crate and scatter across the floor like popcorn.

Jordan gasped. "It's some kind of gun?"

Allan brushed away enough of the packing material to reveal the broad, circular magazine at the top of the weapon, the long barrel and the wooden butt end.

"What kind of gun is this? It looks way too big and awkward for a person to carry," Jordan said, helping remove more of the peanuts.

Allan leaned back on his haunches and opened his palms to present his new artifact. "This, my darling daughter, is an original British WWI Lewis Aircraft Gun Modified for WWII Home Guard with 97-Round Drum Magazine." He slapped his hands on his thighs with satisfaction and whistled. "Ain't she a beauty?"

"You bought a *machine gun?*"

A look of false insult crossed his face. His voice was reverent. "Nooooooooo, this is not just a machine gun…"

Jordan made beckoning motions with the fingers of both

hands as though taunting an opponent to box. "Okay, let me have it…"

"This Lewis gun represents the first model of machine gun ever fired from an aircraft-"

"In the year…"

"On June 7-"

"Of course you know the day…"

"1912, U.S. Captain Charles Chandler fired this prototype," Allan tapped all five fingertips on the gun's magazine, "from the foot-bar of a Wright Model B Flyer." Allan pointed at one of the small model airplanes on a shelf that was full of them. "Note exhibit A."

Jordan spied the envelope taped to the inside wall of the wooden crate and removed it as her father told her more of the artifact's history. She opened the printed pages and scanned the text. "'Rebuilt as totally inert and never to be made operational again,'" she read aloud.

"Of course," Allan said and looked comically regretful. "Can you imagine a State Senator buying a functional antique machine gun? If I was ever found out, it would be a PR nightmare."

Jordan cocked a brow in surprise. "You can buy functional machine guns?"

"Not legally." Allan scratched his chin. "Shoulda been a history prof," he mumbled. "No one cares what a history prof buys."

"Told ya." Jordan went back to reading. "'Often employed for balloon-busting, loaded with incendiary ammunition designed to ignite the hydrogen inside the gasbags of German Zeppelins, other airships and Drache barrage balloons.'" She handed her father the article and patted him on the shoulder as she got to her feet. "Nice one, Dad. Have fun setting it up."

Allan clapped his hands together and rubbed them with glee. "Sure you don't want to help your old man polish it?"

Jordan laughed. "I'll contribute by bringing you some rags and a glass of iced tea." She headed for the door, but stopped and turned back. "By the way, Maria stopped by this morning."

Allan looked up at his daughter. "Really?" He smiled at the mention of Jordan's nanny of years past. "How is she? Why didn't she stick around? I would like to have seen her, too."

Jordan crossed her arms over her chest. "Actually, it was really weird. She came to say goodbye; she's moving back to Belize."

Allan's smile faded. "For good? And she didn't want to see me?"

"I don't think it was a matter of want. It seemed like she was in a rush and-" Jordan paused, wondering if she should express her suspicions out loud.

"What?" he pressed.

"Well, it sort of seemed like she wanted to get out of here before you came back. You guys haven't had a tiff, have you?"

"A tiff?" He dropped his chin, his face incredulous. "We've never fought. Even while she lived here all those years, raising you." He blinked. "Well, now I'm just hurt."

"I'm wondering if it has something to do with this..." Jordan fished the locket out of her pocket and dangled it in front of her dad.

When Allan's eyes fell on the silver locket, his face froze in shock. He took the locket and held it in his palm. "Where did you get this?"

"Maria gave it to me." Jordan didn't like the look on her father's face. "You recognize it?"

Allan ran a hand through his hair and rubbed the back of his neck. "Of course. Your mother bought this locket on our honeymoon from an antique store in Paris. She went crazy as soon as she saw it; she loved the craftsmanship. She had always planned to get our photos done up tiny so she could put them inside."

"On top of the painting?" Jordan raised an eyebrow. "Or did she just change her mind?"

"What painting?" Allan looked confused. "What do you mean?"

"Over the portrait inside."

Allan opened the locket and stared down at the portrait of Jaclyn with disbelief.

"Dad?" Jordan watched Allan's complexion turn waxy. "Are you okay?"

"This is impossible," Allan said. "This locket was always empty." He looked up at his daughter. "When she bought it, it was blank inside."

Jordan frowned. "I guess she changed her mind about what she wanted inside."

Allan rubbed a hand across his brow in agitation. "This makes no sense." Allan fumbled in his pocket for his phone. He scrolled through his contacts with shaking fingers.

"If you're calling Maria, I already tried. Her phone has been disconnected."

Allan pressed dial anyway and held the phone to his ear. After hearing the recording, he hung up. "What did she say when she gave it to you, Jordy?" Allan asked, a sharp line between his brows. "I mean her exact words."

"Dad, you're scaring me."

Allan shook his head. "You don't need to be scared," he said. But Jordan thought the fact that he looked like he'd seen a ghost betrayed the opposite. "Just tell me what she said."

"She didn't say anything about it, Dad. She wouldn't even let me open it while she was still here. She told me to wait until after she left. Why do you think she would do that?"

Allan closed the locket and rubbed a thumb over the silver, thinking. "It explains why she didn't want to cross paths with me. I wish she would have come to *me* with this, instead of giving it to you."

"Why?"

When Allan didn't answer right away, Jordan fought back her frustration. She knelt down next to him and took the locket from his hand. "Dad, talk to me. You're always trying to protect me, but

I'm grown up now. It hurts that you don't trust me. We are all that is left of the Kacy family. If we're not on the same side, then we're alone."

Allan looked at his daughter and couldn't help but marvel at how much she had matured in the last few years. "When did you get so wise?" he mused. When Jordan didn't answer, he took a breath and went on. "When your mother bought this locket, it was blank inside. I promise you that."

"When was the last time you saw it?" The hair on Jordan's arms stood up at the look on her father's face.

Allan paused, then ploughed forward. "Your mother was wearing it when she disappeared the first time."

CHAPTER 6

Jordan couldn't believe her ears. She shook her head. "What do you mean 'the first time'? There was another time when she vanished?" She gripped the locket so tightly that the clasp bit into the flesh of her thumb.

Allan sighed. "Yes."

Jordan waited for him to go on; when he didn't, she grabbed his bicep. "Dad, this is huge. Why didn't you ever tell me?"

"You didn't need to know," Allan answered. "You weren't even alive at the time and it's not important anymore."

Jordan's face flushed with heat. "Bullshit!" she snapped. "Bullshit, 'it's not important'. Bullshit, I didn't 'need to know'."

"Jordy-" Allan said and put a hand over hers in an effort to placate her.

"This is a paradigm shift, dad!" She pulled her hand away, her voice rising. "How could you leave this out? In a missing persons case, this is-" she struggled for the right words. "This is *critical* information. It changes everything." She put her hands over her face and shook her head. "You're unbelievable," she said through her fingers. "Really, I'm just-" she took her hands away, the imprint of her fingers still on her cheeks, "disgusted."

Allan's brow furrowed. "This is why I haven't told you, Jordy. You get too involved emotionally-"

"She's my MOTHER!" Jordan yelled.

"She LEFT!" Allan yelled back.

Jordan's eyes narrowed. "How dare you," she seethed. "How dare you decide what I get to know about my own family? How dare you deny me the facts, especially when you have watched me hunt so hard for them over the years?" Her voice grew hard and Allan began to wilt. "How dare you keep things from me that could help me make sense of the tragedy of this family? Do you realize how selfish you've been?"

Allan's phone rang and he jumped and scrambled to answer it; like it was a lifeline, thrown from a ship to a drowning man. "Hello, hello?"

Frustrated air whistled from between Jordan's teeth. She took off her glasses and rubbed her eyes, willing herself to be patient.

Allan got up off the floor and turned his back to Jordan. "Marcus, I'm here. What is it?"

Jordan rolled her eyes heavenward and put her glasses back on. Marcus was Allan's secretary and he never called on weekends unless it was an emergency. "Thanks, Marcus," Jordan grumbled, "nice timing."

"Well, did you call him?" Allan was saying, then a pause. "I realize that, but-" More dead air. "No, you're right. Of course. I'll go in person. Today-"

Jordan threw her hands up and got to her feet. She crossed her arms and waited for her father to get off the phone.

"Yes, alright. I'm on my way," Allan finished. He hung up and turned to face his daughter, sheepishly. "I have to go."

"Of course you do."

"Don't treat me like I asked for this, Jordy," Allan said, retrieving his jacket from where he'd draped it—over the chair that Ernest King had sat in while he was Chief of Naval Operations during WWII. "We'll talk when I get back. It's probably a good idea for you to cool off, anyway."

Jordan clenched her jaw. "Allan," she said, quietly.

Her father turned back to her in surprise. She'd never called him by his name.

"When you get back, we're going to sit down and you're going to tell me everything." She moved closer to him and glared into his face. Allan took a step back from the woman who used to be his little princess. "Every. Little. Thing. I mean it," Jordan blinked up at him through her glasses. She pushed her specs up her nose. "You and I are all we have left. We have each other, that's it. Unless you want to lose me too, you'll spill it all and you'll do it tonight."

Allan paled and the column of his throat moved as he swallowed. "Even if it makes you hate her?"

It was Jordan's turn to pause and consider something new. Allan could see the cogs turning in his daughter's brain. She heard him. She processed it. She rejected the notion. "That's impossible." Jordan's answer was resolute.

Allan touched Jordan's cheek and nodded tightly. He turned and left the room and as he was descending the wide staircase to the foyer, he said under his breath, "That's how I felt, too."

CHAPTER 7

Jordan listened from her father's war room as the Land Rover's engine turned over and the vehicle drove away. She put her hands to her cheeks where anger had made them hot and red. Her heart was still pounding with indignation. Maybe Allan was right; she needed to cool off before she could sit and listen to what he had to say without blowing a fuse. She needed the oak. *Her* oak and the swing Allan had made for her when she was fifteen. Before then, it had been a tire swing, but she felt too old for the tire swing, so Allan had surprised her, on her birthday, with an elegant wooden bench for two. On that swinging bench, she had sat with her grandparents before they'd passed away. She'd sat with her dad and wiled away hot Sunday afternoons. She'd sat with Maria on humid evenings, listening to the crickets. But most of all, she'd sat there by herself —reading, studying, or just thinking.

Jordan took the narrow servants' stairs down to the kitchen and went out through the back door. The estate used to be twelve hundred acres, but Allan had long ago severed the agricultural land and sold it off to developers as the suburbs crept further west, leaving them fifty acres of private land. The backyard was sprawling and green. Cal kept the shrubs manicured, the roses trained and a small garden cultivated for Jordan to pick vegetables and herbs. But the property's claim to fame was the towering, centuries-old oaks. Jordan thought of them as gentle giants and guardians. Her oak was in the middle of the back lawn; its trunk so thick it would require five men to grab hands, just to wrap all the way around it. With its fat, gnarling limbs sprawled wide and the canopy overhead thick and healthy, the oak was a majestic sight. The wooden swing looked like a child's toy, dangling from the branches.

Jordan crossed the lawn in her bare feet, locket in hand and sat on the bench. Letting it sway, she tucked her feet up under her and tilted her head back. The sky was barely visible through the thick canopy of the 500-year-old tree. Her oak had survived lightning, flooding, pestilence and the hacking off of huge limbs. Whatever it experienced, it always came back stronger and more beautiful.

Jordan knew about the intelligence of plants and trees. Water drawn up through the tree's roots vibrated at a frequency proven to be restorative to humans. Being close enough to a tree of this age and strength helped her take on the same frequency. It was like hitting her reboot button, triggering healing. After sitting near her giant and feeling the calm that came over her, Jordan could finally believe it.

She again took her mother's locket out of her pocket and rubbed her thumb over its silver face. She frowned and clenched the locket tight. *Is it vibrating?* Jordan jerked upright on the bench, setting it swaying. She stared down at the locket, aghast. *It is vibrating!*

"What the hell?!" Jordan got to her feet, holding the locket away from her. There was a sound, very faint, like the buzzing from a hive of bees. The locket was humming. Jordan clamped a hand over her mouth. *It's impossible. I'm imagining it.* She put the locket down on the bench, pushed her glasses up on her nose and stared at it. The sound of the vibration grew louder and the locket buzzed against the wood. It began to jump and jiggle. "What is going on?" Jordan cried, her hands flying to her cheeks. Every nerve was struck, every hair on her body erect.

A louder buzzing sound, like electricity sparking, made her look up into the oak's branches. Jordan gave a cry and took a step backward, tripping and landing on her tailbone in the grass. She didn't even feel the pain. A bright web of sparks flashed between the branches of the oak, snapping and humming like a power cable. Lines of them swept up and into the limbs, one after the other, dissipating into the thick leaves. Flickering and popping, some of the lines made a small ring that did not dissipate, but held steady, buzzing loudly. Connecting two of the oak's limbs, it made an enclosed circle. The shape shrank and then grew and in the center…

Jordan got to her feet and adjusted her glasses with trembling fingers. She squinted, her eyes unable to make sense of what she was seeing. In the center, she thought she could see more branches, but they were at odd angles, criss-crossing over the hole. Those branches were clearly not part of her oak tree.

A scream tore from Jordan's throat as something flew through the ring of sparks at a terrifying speed, crashing into the oak with a loud snap of breaking branches. The humming lines of electricity vanished and the oak went silent. A dark mass remained in the crotch of the trunk, propped against a thick limb.

Jordan's chest rose and fell rapidly, her heart hammered in her chest and her body cried out for oxygen. She craned her neck up to look at the oak and whatever had hit it. She screamed again when something swung down from the mass and dangled before hanging still. The 'something' that dangled had fingers. Her heart pounding like she'd just sprinted for her life, Jordan took a few steps closer to the tree. Bending her head back until her neck spasmed, she strained her eyes, trying to glimpse what she could. Her vision was terrible, but with her glasses, she could see as well as most people. *It is a hand; I'm not imagining it. And the hand is attached to a forearm, which has to be attached to a human. Right?*

Jordan's brain felt scrambled. She was at a complete and utter loss; she didn't know what to do next and paralysis rammed her in the chest. A man had flown out of nowhere and hit her oak tree – possibly hard enough to kill him. Sweat gathered in the hollow of her back and trickled down her spine. She had to do something. *What if he is still alive? He'll be injured and if he dies because I'm standing here like a fungus... But where the hell did he come from?* She shook her head and steeled herself. *If he's alive, I can ask him.* She put a hand out and clutched the rung of the wooden ladder her father had nailed into the tree over fifteen years ago—a ladder which helped a young girl who was fond of climbing get up into the tree. She prayed the rungs would still hold and began to climb.

"Hello?" Jordan called as she put hand over hand and pulled herself up. The rungs were soft and a bit slimy and cool against her bare feet in spite of the heat of the day. There was no response to her call. She kept climbing.

"I'm coming up to help you," she said, just in case the person was able to hear her. "Help is on the way." She was speaking just as much to comfort herself as the stranger who was either dead or dying in her tree.

"Hang tight," she said, giving a borderline hysterical laugh at the unintentional pun. She clenched her eyes tight for a second. "Get a grip, Jordan."

The sound of fabric ripping, followed by that of something heavy sliding against the bark, made her gasp and peer around the trunk. The dangling arm had shifted lower and was joined by the shape of a head and then a shoulder. Hair hung down toward the earth. The thickness and the shape of the body made her certain the 'something' was a man. A man with longish hair.

"No. No, no, no," Jordan intoned, climbing faster.

The body slid slowly, almost languidly, over the branch and toward the ground.

Jordan fully extended her arm, groaning in the effort to reach him. It wasn't enough. Her fingertips just brushed the skin of his bare arm as he gained speed and dropped from the branch. Jordan winced as the man hit a limb on the way down and then another, before landing on the grass at the foot of the oak with a dull *thud*.

"This isn't happening." Jordan peered down at the heap of arms and legs now on the ground beneath her. "This is crazy. I'm crazy. I've finally cracked." She reversed her direction, back down the tree. She mimicked Allan's voice as she descended. "Oh, sorry I forgot to mention. Your mother disappeared once before. Sorry about that, just slipped my mind." Rung by slippery rung she went. "That's alright, Dad," she went on with her little made-up dialogue, "it's just all I needed to become completely unhinged. Did you know that our oak tree is a semiconductor and can-" She stopped blathering when she dropped onto the ground, landing in a crouch next to the man.

With eyes as big as plates, Jordan took in the sight of the man —noting first the blood flowing freely from the cut above his left eye and then the strange bulge at his right shoulder. His shoulder was dislocated; she'd seen it happen to someone who had been bouldering at the indoor gym. Her next observation was his strange clothing. A brown leather vest that looked butter-soft encased his torso. How he got it on was a mystery. The front of it was made from a single piece of leather and was free from laces, buttons, zippers, or any other way of fastening it. It had seams up the sides under the arms, but they were tightly sewn, with no way to open them except with scissors. Soft leather pants wrapped around long legs and dark green leather boots came to just below his kneecaps. Straps across the front of his chest hung loose and disappeared underneath him. Two thinner straps wrapped around his right thigh, holding a sheath. The hilt of a blade protruded from it. His skin was deeply tanned and his shoulder-length hair was threaded with a few small braids. The top half of his hair was pulled away from his forehead, displaying a high widow's peak.

"Looks like you came off a *Lord of the Rings* set," Jordan muttered. "Let me guess; you're a stuntman and they aimed the catapult in the wrong direction? Poor dear."

Jordan's body finally responded and she darted forward. Something glinted in the grass and she spied the locket where it had fallen from the swing. She snatched it up, feeling that it had now gone quiet. In one motion, she dropped the locket into the chest pocket of her shirt and put her fingers to the man's throat. His pulse was weak, but he was alive.

She bit off a scream at his sudden throaty groan. He mumbled some strange words and she bent to listen, but didn't hear anything that sounded like English. His eyes were still closed.

"What? I'm sorry, I can't understand you." She chewed her lip, wondering what to do. She'd have to call for help, unless he soon woke up and was able stand on his own. There didn't appear to be anything wrong with his legs, but who knew? He could have broken every bone in his body, the way he hit the tree.

His eyelids fluttered and Jordan caught a glimpse of the iciest blue between his lashes. He gave a tortured moan and opened his eyes, but just barely.

"Hello," Jordan said, feeling stupid. "I think you've dislocated your shoulder."

His crystal-colored eyes tracked her through half-closed lids. "English," he croaked in a strange accent. He coughed and then inquired, "England?"

"Uh, America," she answered. *He thinks he's in England?* Jordan felt adrenalin flood her limbs. Everything in her believed his question was authentic, but how could he be so lost?

He coughed again and lifted a brown hand to his shoulder. He groaned and one shoulder rose off the dirt as he twisted to try and get up. He clenched his teeth and let out a long growl of agony.

"Maybe you shouldn't move." Jordan put a hand out, but didn't touch him.

His face seemed to register some thought and he looked down; his eyes widened, as though he was looking for something important. His left hand found the straps across his chest and he reached around behind him with another loud grunt of pain. Then he leaned forward and Jordan saw his fingers grasp at a leather satchel that he shifted out from underneath him. He sighed in relief and flopped onto his back, keeping a hand on the satchel.

Jordan hovered at his side, not sure what to do with her hands. Her maternal instinct was kicking in and the desire to fix him up was growing fast and making her fingers twitch. But his foreign dress, his somewhat barbaric appearance, the accent she couldn't place and the faintly dangerous air about him; all of these things stayed her hand. He was exceptionally lean and his arms were vascular. Broad shoulders, slim hips and long legs made him look like some kind of athlete. A touch of sunburn on his nose and forehead and deeply golden skin, belied hours spent outside. "How do you feel?" Jordan asked.

"Like I hit a tree," he said in thickly-accented English. His voice was a deep rasp. Jordan wondered if it always sounded like that, or if he was sick. He put a questing hand on his right ribcage and probed there. He twisted to rise up again and this time he made it all the way to sitting. "I wonder," he said and then looked up at her, "if you might help me to stand?"

"Of course," she said. "But your shoulder-"

"I can put it back in," he said. "But I need to stand."

"Okay." She patted her shoulder and he put a hand on it. "I'm stronger than I look," she said. "Put your weight on me."

He gave a wheezing groan as he got to his feet. The bulge at his right shoulder looked worse when he was standing. The color in the man's face faded and he swayed on his feet. Jordan steadied him.

"If you tell me what to do, I can help," she suggested.

He grimaced, his face twisting into a one-eyed mask of pain. "Take my wrist and when I say to, help me lift my arm up quickly. The shoulder joint needs to go back into place."

Jordan faced him and took his right wrist. "Ready when you are."

He gave a coughing sound that almost sounded like a laugh. His icy blue eyes met her teal ones and she thought he might have smiled through his pain. "Three, two-"

They lifted together on "one," and he bellowed and staggered, then bent over at the waist and groaned through clenched teeth.

That's when Jordan saw the short spears tucked into a small case at his back. Small silver blades fell from somewhere and scattered across the grass. Her eyes widened and she stepped back from him. "What are those for?"

He scooped them up and tucked them back into the small case. "Insurance," he groaned. As he straightened, the remaining pink drained from his cheeks and his eyes drifted shut.

Jordan stepped under him, half catching him as he fell. "Don't pass out again. Can you walk?"

He took a staggering step and the two made their way to the house like some strange injured beast. Jordan's hand shifted across his back and her fingers slid into a tear in the back of the man's vest. Finding her palm on bare skin, she gasped. He glanced down at her and his mouth seemed to quirk.

Did I do something funny? She held the back door open for him and got a glimpse of the back of his vest. More weirdness.

His vest wasn't torn. Two long seams ran down his back from the top of his shoulders all the way down to the bottom of the vest. The top and bottom of each seam were criss-crossed with leather stitching and tied. The center of each seam was open and she could see his shoulder blades through them. She narrowed her eyes and cocked her head. *What purpose could those strange openings possibly serve?*

Jordan helped him through the kitchen and into the parlor, where she deposited him on the sofa with a grunt.

"Just a few minutes' rest," he said.

"I think you'll need a bit more than that," Jordan said. She went to the kitchen and filled a glass with water. Rummaging in the junk drawer, she grabbed a bottle of ibuprofen. The last things she grabbed before leaving the kitchen were an ice pack from the freezer and a clean cloth and bandage for the cut on his forehead. By the time Jordan had gotten back, the man had removed his leather bags and dropped them to the carpet beside him. He was lying with his right arm at his side, inert and his left forearm over his forehead. His eyes were open and focused on Jordan when she entered.

"What is your name?" he asked.

"Jordan," she crossed the carpet and set the drugs and the glass of water on the table near the couch. "And you?"

"Sol."

There was an awkward moment when they just stared at each other. *Are we supposed to shake hands?* she wondered. But Sol made no move to hold out a hand.

"And what did you do, Jordan?" was his next question. His face was pale but his eyes were sharp, appraising.

"I got you some water and some ice," she said. "And something for the pain."

"No, I mean, where am I and how did I get here?"

There was something in his tone that made Jordan frown. *Is he accusing me of something?* "Put this on your shoulder," Jordan said, handing him the ice pack. She ignored his tone and answered him with what she knew. "You are in the state of Virginia, not far outside of Richmond. How you got here?" She shrugged. "I was hoping you could tell me that."

"Were you messing with a portal?" he asked, slapping the ice onto his shoulder.

Jordan blinked. Her hand brushed against the locket in her pocket as she remembered the way it had jumped and hummed. Jordan felt the blood drain from her face and she sat in the chair at the end of the sofa. "A portal? Like a door? In a tree? What?" *But there isn't any such thing as portals. And portals to where?* But deep inside, she knew he wasn't making it up. The string of sparks, the snapping electricity, they way he'd come out of nowhere. It was the only thing that made sense. *Except it's crazy. Isn't it?*

She felt his eyes on her, calculating. "You blundered it open, didn't you." It wasn't a question. He rubbed his left hand over his face. "Great," he said into his hand. He ran his hand down his face and tugged on his chin. "What were you doing right before the portal opened?"

Jordan wasn't sure what to say. *Will he want to take the locket away from me if I tell him? But he seems to have the answers...* "I was holding my mother's locket in my hand…" she trailed off.

"Did it hum?" he asked.

She nodded.

"Let me see it," he held out a hand.

"I'd rather not," she said. "It's important to me and I don't know you."

He gestured wide at the situation with his uninjured arm. "I'm in pain and laying on your couch. I'm not interested in stealing your relic. I just need to go back."

Jordan hesitated, but then reached into her shirt pocket and pulled out the locket. She held it up by the chain so he could see it.

"Put it in my palm," he said. "I won't take it from you."

She got up and stood over him, dangling the locket where he could reach it. She kept a firm grip on the chain.

His brown hand closed around the locket and he held it for

several seconds before letting it go. He nodded. "Where did you get it?"

"My nanny gave it to me earlier today." She returned to the chair, dropping the locket back into the pocket on the front of her shirt.

"Your nanny?" He looked surprised.

"From when I was little, not now."

His eyes darted to the doorway. "Is she here now?"

"No, she-" Jordan's forearms prickled with goosebumps. "She's unreachable."

CHAPTER 8

"Go back where?" Jordan asked, eyeing the leather satchels and the quiver of small spears on her carpet. "Pardon me?"

"You said you 'just need to go back'; go back where?"

"Oriceran," he said and, after a breath, "Do you have any idea how dangerous it is to open a portal?" he asked. "People die doing that. Or worse."

She blinked. "Worse than die?"

He shifted on the couch. Jordan noticed a fine sheen of sweat on his forehead. "And it's bloody inconvenient," he mumbled. He reached for the water, downed the entire glass and set the soles of his boots on the floor as he sat upright. He set the ice pack on the table, grunted and got to his feet. He swayed there. His face looked drawn, disoriented. For a moment, he looked as though he could be any age – twenty, fifty, one hundred.

"Are you sure you should–" Jordan began.

He fell forward onto the carpet, limply, landing face-first with a *thump*. His arms were underneath him and his face was pressed into the floor. His back arched and those strange slashes in his vest gaped, showing the smooth skin and muscle underneath.

"Stand?" Jordan finished. She bent over his lumpy form, grasped his shoulder and pulled. With effort, she rolled him over; his forearms and hands untwisted and brushed against her chest as she put him on his back. "I'm just going to leave you here," she said, even though he clearly couldn't hear her. "I'm going to call for help and I'll be back. Maybe my dad will know what to do with you."

She put the icepack on Sol's forehead; the cut over his eye had begun leaking again. She blotted it with a tissue and left the room to find her phone. The manor hadn't had a landline in years. Who needed a landline when cell phones were so much more convenient?

She went up the stairs two at a time to her father's memorabilia room, where she'd last seen her phone. She crossed the room to where she left it sitting on a library shelf, but froze when she heard the sound of the squeaky floorboard. She gasped and listened. Her hand flew to her empty chest pocket.

"Sol!" she belted, furious. He'd tricked her. The bum had taken her locket, fainting as a ruse. Her face flushed with heat, as much with embarrassment as with anger. The kitchen screen door slammed. Jordan bolted from her room, her phone forgotten. In her bare feet, she ran down the stairs, through the kitchen and out the back door. She flew across the back deck like an angel from Revelations; her eyes alight. She picked up a couple of splinters from the heat-baked wood on her way. Sol was already halfway across the yard; a glint of light off the locket dangling from his fist confirmed what he'd done like a soft slap in the face. She sprinted after him, now on the grass, making it lie down and bleed under her heels. Her head pounded with effort. She would be less angry if he'd stolen money, but steal a locket with a handpainted picture of her mother inside?

Sol glanced back as the door behind Jordan slammed shut, then picked up the pace and ran for the tree, his gait stiff. Jordan increased her speed, her teeth clenched, as the gap closed between him and the tree. The snapping of electricity could already be heard as the two raced for the oak.

"Drop the locket," Jordan yelled. "Go, but drop the locket first!"

Sol's fist did not loosen. He looked back and saw Jordan closing in on him fast and his eyes widened. "Stop, Jordan!" The yellow sparks were sweeping up the tree branches and the bark was flickering and full of miniature, exploding stars. Sol spun his back to the oak and threw the locket at Jordan, straight at her face. Sol could see her looming teal eyes before him and feel the heat of the sparking portal behind him.

Putting her fist up, as fast as a striking snake, she caught the necklace, but not before she barrelled into him. Reflexively, Sol's arms closed around her as she knocked the wind out of him and the two of them fell onto the roots of the oak.

Jordan's vision went black and the humming of an electric current became so loud her molars buzzed in the back of her head. She tried to scream and felt the tearing of sound at her throat, but she couldn't hear her own cries. There was no sound but the zapping and humming of some giant, unrepentant monster made of energy. The pressure of the air increased, pressing in from every side, tightening, squeezing. Just when she thought that her very bones would grind into powder and her joints would break, the pressure and the sound of electricity died a sudden death. For a second, she heard the sound of whispering voices, thousands of them, all speaking over each other with urgency. They grew louder, none of them with any discernible words. Then they, too, stopped. Suddenly and finitely, there was a welcome silence.

A flash of bright light illuminated a blurred scene of green and blue and a sickening drop made her stomach vault into her mouth. She felt the ground come up under her feet, but too fast and at a strange angle. Her legs buckled and she fell, landing on her shoulder. The air *whoosh*ed out of her in a whacking gust and her body flipped over her head, her neck cracking and something popping. Momentum carried her and the ground dropped away beneath her like a bad joke, the angle growing sharper. She tumbled faster. Light and dark flashed by. She was jabbed, poked, bruised; everything was a blur of soft colors of sky and ground. She registered the sound of Sol thudding and grunting as he tumbled along beside her. *Will we ever stop?* Jordan thought when her hip clipped something unforgiving. Her hands flailed for purchase, but felt only the passing of plant stalks and twigs as she rolled by them like a stone more than happy to pick up speed.

"Ooof!" Jordan's back slammed up against something solid, meaty. The acrid, horrific stench of rot filled her nostrils and nausea came up swiftly like a punch in the throat. Dizzy and bruised, but finally no longer falling, she put a hand out to brace herself on something, anything that would make her world come to a standstill. It landed on something bristly and rough, like the skin of an elephant. A shapeless blob of dark matter whirled by her vision, like her eyeballs had been replaced by the googly kind found in the heads of dolls.

She pushed against the blob in an effort to stand and heard a sound like a soft fart. She managed to get her body positioned over her feet, though her weight wanted to slide forward and fall into whatever had ended her rolling.

Miraculously, the locket was still clutched in her hand. She almost had to pry her own fingers open, so tightly they'd been clenched around it. She stuffed the locket into the pocket of her jean shorts.

A cloud of reeking wind drifted by her nose and Jordan gagged and spat. Her mouth watered, telegraphing the possibility of forthcoming vomit. The world was still spinning. Jordan swayed and bent down. She crawled on her hands and knees away from the farting thing, making a crooked path through the shrubs and dry grasses along the steep hillside. The smell was so pungent, Jordan's eyes filled with water and tears coursed down her cheeks. She gagged again and tried to get to her feet. Slowly, the world was ceasing its spin.

With great effort, Jordan stood. Everything hurt and the world was a blur. Her hands flew to her face where she found no glasses to aid her.

"Sol?" Fear lurched into her heart like a beast from a nightmare. She couldn't survive without her glasses and nothing around her was familiar. She took a deep breath and closed her eyes. "Stay calm," she coached herself. "Deep breaths." She took a breath, but only gagged again. When she opened her eyes, the world wasn't quite as blurry. In fact, the reeking thing that had stopped her fall was starting to take shape.

Its details slowly came into focus as Jordan squinted at the carcass. It was massive, the size of a bull elephant—maybe bigger. But she couldn't make out its features, as it lay with its back to her. Its skin was a shade of brown, bristly with stiff hair and was stretched tautly over a mound of ribs. A strip of shaggy hair lay scraggly on the back of its neck.

Jordan staggered around the thing, horror slipping its cold fingers around her. Horror that she'd landed against a rotting carcass, but it went deeper than that. It was the kind of terror that dawned slowly, like a sunrise – the warm light illuminating first this, then that. Horror, because she'd never seen an animal like it – with her own eyes, in a picture book, or on any nature documentary. She covered her mouth and nose as her vision grew sharp. She had never really believed it, that there could be a portal to another place.

Oh, yes, she'd seen the tree snap and flicker and send out its showers of sparks. She'd seen a man fly out of nowhere, a man in foreign clothes and with a foreign accent. She'd seen him bleed and helped him put his dislocated shoulder back into place.

But we're told all kinds of things as we grow up.

A fat man in a red suit squeezes himself and a bunch of pre-wrapped presents down your chimney once a year. A fairy with gossamer wings and a tutu loves to collect your baby teeth and will even pay you for them. Yes, she'll leave a silver coin under your pillow while you dream. If you squash your face together so your lips pop out fatly and you hold it for too long, your face will never go back to normal.

We're told all kinds of things like that. But the uncharted beast before her, this great corpse, was not of Earth. Not of her world. And seeing it kicked her in the teeth with its truth. *Welcome! Come on in! Come be part of the greatest show on earth,* it seemed to bray into her mind, laughing with the rich and resonant tones of a showman.

A strangled "No" was all that slipped out, as what Jordan was seeing played across her mind.

Huge, ragged gashes across the animal's side were open and crawling with maggots. Its four eyes had sunk into its massive head, which also had four tusks and a line of hair down the center of its face, to four big nostrils crusted with dried blood. She stepped around hoofs the size of manhole covers. More gashes across its gut. Intestines spilled out onto the grass and a dark shadowy hole gaped at its belly. Jordan turned her head just in time to spew onto the scrubby grass beside her. Spitting and gasping, she stayed on her hands and knees until she caught her breath. She passed a hand over her face and mouth.

"Sol!" she screamed again with gusto. She got to her feet and backed away from the carcass. *Is that the sound of waves behind me?* She turned and caught the sight of a stretch of blue.

But the sound of something wet and juicy and much closer made her turn back. Something the size of a cat and armed with pincers and mandibles appeared from the cavity of the dead beast. It made a loud hissing *clack*; its eyes, on the ends of upright stems, darted around independently of one another until they both landed on her. Jordan screamed in terror. She stepped back, her arms flailing and lost her footing on the steep ground. Landing on her butt on a downward slope, the momentum carried her body over and she tumbled again, continuing on her journey downward.

"Oooof!" Air whooshed out of Jordan as she landed with her hand under her stomach and was flipped onto her back. She slid down an embankment, ploughing up sand in front her before finally coming to a stop. The sound of waves was louder now. She craned her aching neck and saw water lapping at a small beach not far from her. She groaned and rolled over onto her stomach. *At least the air doesn't reek of rotting meat here and whatever that horrid beast was didn't chase me down to the water's edge.*

She got to her hands and knees, sand cascading from her clothes and hair. She brushed herself off, groaning at the hundred bruises forming from head to toe. A dull headache throbbed in her left temple. She rubbed her eyes and remembered that she'd lost her glasses. She froze and then pulled her hands away from her face to look around.

She could see the scrubby grass poking up through the sand beneath her. She could see the foam in the waves as the water pushed up the beach, only to drop away again. She could see the winged shapes of birds as they flapped and climbed up over the treetops along the distant shore. She could *see*. She lost track of time as she stood there in awe, taking in the world around her without the assistance of spectacles.

A dark shape darted from the shadow of a bush draped with vines. Jordan gasped. A crab the size of a coffee table scuttled across the sand and headed straight for her. Its flat, gray shell was ringed with nasty looking horns and one snapping claw was twice the size of the other. It moved way too fast. *That claw could cut my leg off!*

Jordan shrieked again and began to run up the sandy embankment. Looking back over her shoulder, she saw a second giant crab join in on the pursuit. Her toes ploughed into the deep sand, slowing her getaway. "Where the hell are you, Sol?!" She screamed as she scrambled. A sharp *snip* sounded behind her, like massive pinking shears, ready to cut her in half. *This is it. This is how I'm going to die. Dinner for overgrown crabs. A crab cake,* she thought, irrationally.

Something whizzed by her head and a *thud* made her turn. The first crab collapsed with a short spear buried in its face, right between its eyestalks. The second crab passed its fallen comrade without notice or concern, its claws and mandibles waving menacingly. Jordan squealed and doubled her efforts to get away. Panic overtook her and she tripped in the sand, falling to her knees.

Sol appeared over the bluff, carrying a tree branch. He ran past Jordan lifting it like a golfer preparing to swing a club. As the crab closed in with its huge, razor-sharp pincer opened and aimed for Sol's shin, Sol lifted his leg out of pinching range and swung, hard.

Snap! Thwack!

The claw closed around air as Sol struck the crab with the branch, hitting it in the mandibles and lifting the front four legs of the heavy crustacean right off the ground. Its legs scrabbled at the air before it fell back to the sand. It closed both its pincers over its face and reversed direction, scuttling sideways into the water and disappearing under the waves.

Jordan lay there in shock, buried up to her forearms in sand, panting hard, her chest heaving. Sweat trickled down the side of her face and she pushed her hair back, leaving a sandy streak on her forehead. She rolled over onto her elbows and put a hand to her pounding heart. With her eyes as wide as saucers, she watched Sol approach the dead crab and pull the spear out of its face. It came out with a sucking sound.

"Monster... crabs..." Jordan panted.

"Those were the babies," Sol said matter-of-factly. Jordan's stomach folded in on itself, writhing like a salted leech. *How big are the mommy and daddy crabs, then?* The thought had her scrambling to her feet, though her legs were quaking. Her eyes scanned the water for signs of a Volkswagen-sized crab.

Sol reached down, picked up the dead crab's big claw with both hands and twisted it until it made a cracking sound. Then he twisted it the other way, grunting with the effort – or maybe with the pain of his recently dislocated shoulder.

Jordan winced as the nausea gave an encore at the back of her throat. "What are you doing?"

Sol rotated the claw around and around; snapping and popping sounds filled the air when the limb finally broke free. He picked up the busted claw and put it over his good shoulder, where it hung and dripped ooze into the sand behind him.

"Dinner," he growled and stalked past her.

CHAPTER 9

"Ouch, dammit!" Jordan hopped on one foot and plucked a thorn from the side of her big toe. She'd been following Sol and the oozing claw for fifteen minutes across sharply angled, scrubby hillside. A green line of forest had appeared in the distance. Already, her feet were bleeding from half a dozen cuts. She was in shock. Her mind was in a fog and there were so many questions in her brain that they jammed up in her brain like a pileup on a freeway. Sol ignored her cry of pain.

"Shouldn't we be heading uphill? Back to the portal?" Jordan called at his back.

Sol didn't turn and didn't answer.

"I'd like to be back before my dad gets home, if possible."

Sol halted, seemingly frozen to the spot.

"What?" Jordan stopped as well and took the opportunity to remove a weed from between her toes. The evening sun was hot and surprisingly blinding and she blinked at him in the light. If it was so warm this late in the day, what would it be like at high noon?

Slowly, Sol turned to face her. The claw swung around like

the arm of a construction crane, a line of slime swinging from it. The slime drooled onto the ground with a *plop*.

Jordan straightened. "You look upset."

A screaming roar in the distance made Sol's eyes dart upward. "Keep walking." He turned and continued along the hillside. The giant claw cast a long, strange shadow behind him.

"What was that?" Jordan scampered to catch up, dodging the sharp stalks of scrubby grass that poked up from the sandy soil. She caught a whiff of pungent air and staggered back, her hand going to her nose. "Dude, that claw stinks."

Sol mumbled something incomprehensible and kept walking.

"Why are we going *away* from the portal?"

No response.

Her face flushed with annoyance. *Does he have to be such a jerk? Why isn't he telling me anything?* He obviously had ideas about where they needed to be, but whatever those ideas were, they took the pair in the opposite direction of where Jordan thought they needed to be. Jordan stopped walking and put her hands on her hips, thinking. She watched Sol continue to walk away from her and from the hill they'd tumbled down.

"Fine, I'll go back on my own." Jordan turned and began heading uphill. "So rude," she muttered. "I have the locket, now. I don't need you."

"That feroth carcass was a harpy kill," Sol called over his shoulder. "If you'd like to be dessert, by all means, keep going that way."

Jordan froze. *A harpy kill?* The image of the massive gashes in the body rose to her mind. She turned back to her prickly companion. "A harpy? Body of a bird, head of a woman, three boobs? That kind of harpy?" She wouldn't have believed it, except that she'd already seen enough wildlife in this place to last her a lifetime. She had no desire to add a harpy to the mix.

Sol gave a humorless laugh and shook his head. "Yeah, just like that." His words were laced with sarcasm.

Jordan caught up to Sol, getting as close as she could without having to smell the ooze from the dismembered crab claw.

"Can you at least tell me what your plan is? Cuz from what I can see, we're getting further and further from the doorway that will take me away from this crazy, dangerous place. My dad is going to worry when he gets home and sees I'm not there." She added to herself, "Our family has had enough of people randomly disappearing without a trace."

"You should have thought of that before you pushed us both through the portal," Sol replied with a nonchalance that made Jordan feel cold. "You won't be going home today, or tomorrow, or possibly for quite a while." He shook his head again. "Earthlings," he muttered.

Jordan froze the spot. "What did you say?"

Another hair-raising scream in the distance made her wince and look over her shoulder.

"Pick up the pace, Jordan," Sol said and showed her what kind of pace he meant. "We need to get as far from here as we can before nightfall."

Jordan clenched her jaw and began to jog on her sore and naked feet.

By the time they reached the trees over an hour later, Jordan was limping. A softer trail of ferns and grasses opened up between the trees and Jordan breathed a sigh of relief to be off the scrubby hillside with its sharp foliage.

Sol hadn't spared her a glance. Anger and annoyance radiated from him. Jordan was accustomed to men falling over themselves for an opportunity to help her; apparently Sol was not a sucker for a pretty face.

"I should have left you to rot in that tree," Jordan muttered as she limped after Sol. "Cretin."

If Sol heard her, he didn't respond.

Several hours later, the sun was nearly down and they were deep into a lush forest full of mushrooms, ferns and moss. Jordan opened her mouth to beg for a break when Sol finally stopped in a small clearing. Jordan limped to a nearby log and wilted down onto it. Picking up one foot to examine the sole and brush away the dirt, she bit off a whimper at the multitude of tiny stinging cuts she uncovered. When she looked up again, the crab claw was on the ground and Sol was nowhere to be seen. She straightened, taking a look around. The sun was nearly set and, this deep into the woods, it was almost too dim to make out the details of their little clearing. She was about to call after Sol when he reappeared.

"There's a spring through there," Sol said, pointing through the trees. His hair and face were damp. He rolled his shoulders and flexed his injured arm. "Wash your feet."

Jordan nodded. "Thanks." She got up and limped in the direction Sol had pointed. Not far into the brush, there was indeed a small stream burbling up from underground. Jordan sat on her butt and dipped a toe in. Sighing at the cool water, Jordan lowered both feet in up to her ankles. She washed off the dirt and massaged her aching muscles. The stinging of multiple cuts and scrapes seemed to ease almost immediately. Amazed, Jordan immersed her hands, too. The pain from the scrapes she'd received from the sharp, hidden stalks as she'd crawled through the sand also seemed to disappear. She scooped a handful of water to her face and tentatively slurped the liquid. It was sweet and slightly minty. Suddenly consumed by thirst, Jordan drank mouthful after mouthful and almost moaned with relief. With each swallow, she could feel vitality returning to her tired limbs.

"Don't drink too much." Sol's voice came from behind her. She turned to see him holding an armful of twigs and branches. In one hand was a nasty looking blade. The sheath at his thigh was empty.

"How come? It tastes amazing and I feel so much better." Jordan flicked water off her hands and stood, still soothing her feet in the stream.

"Too much puutso water can be a hallucinogen to someone who has never had it before." Sol turned and went back to the clearing, where he stooped and began to make a fire.

"Now he tells me," Jordan muttered.

"Puutso water works on suggestion," said Sol as he worked to prepare their dinner. "I would have to tell you something is there before you could see it. But I wouldn't do that to you. Teenagers like to sneak the water to their friends and scare them out of their wits."

"Like being hypnotized," said Jordan, stepping out of the stream.

"Something like that."

Sol had the crab claw skewered and balanced between two Y-shaped sticks that he'd jammed into the earth. He'd arranged his collection of dried wood and twigs into a rough tent-shape. Jordan watched as he took a flint from one of his leather satchels and used it to spark a fire to life. As he blew on the tinder, the flames caught and flared.

Jordan sat on the ground next to the fire, her eyes on Sol as he worked.

"You're quite the survivalist," Jordan said.

Sol's eyes flashed to her, one eyebrow raised and then back down to the fire.

Jordan rolled her eyes and let out a sigh. "Can we talk now, or is it more fun to keep the stupid human in the dark?"

Sol took a breath through his nose and let it out slowly, purposefully. "Ask whatever you want."

"Why did you say I wouldn't be able to go home right away?"

Sol shifted from a squat to sit fully on the ground and turned the claw as the flames licked at it. "Your relic has enough magic to open a portal, but it's a rudimentary magic. If you could even find the portal we came through and not get killed by harpies on the way, there is no guarantee it would take you back to your property. It could spit you out somewhere in

Africa; or worse, your relic could only have enough magic in it to do half the job."

"Half the job?"

"It might get you to the in-between, but no further. In which case you'd be stuck there. You might even leave parts here, while other parts continue through the portal."

Jordan paled. "Parts?"

"Yes, 'parts,'" Sol said. "As in body parts."

"My God. Why didn't you warn me-"

"I tried to," Sol snapped. He rubbed a palm up his forehead and back over his hairline. His eyes bored into her, looking nearly black in the firelight. "Your fiddling around with that locket has cost me my wings and a mountain of time. Who knows what kind of disaster this delay has caused?"

Jordan bit back a stinging retort about how important he must be when his words sank in. "Your *wings*?"

"I'm an Arpak," Sol said, then added, "not that I expect you to know what that is. But, basically, I'm a member of a society of winged humans called Strix. Strix is the genus, Arpak is the species. My wings don't survive portal passages to Earth, as there isn't enough magic in your world to sustain them."

"Those slashes in the back of your vest-"

Sol watched her. "Putting it together now, are you?"

"So, you had wings and they, what… vanished when you went through the portal?"

Sol nodded. "Instantly."

Jordan absorbed this. "If you had told me this was possible yesterday, I would have laughed in your face. But now…" She couldn't deny what her own senses were telling her. There was another dimension, separate from Earth, where creatures considered to be mythological, or not considered at all in her reality, were flesh and blood. Her hand drifted to her mouth as her eyes took in the man before her. "Your wings-" The horrible realization of what he had lost began to sink in. It would be akin to losing both arms. The edges of her vision blurred and for a fraction of a second, Jordan thought she saw huge feathered wings reaching out impossibly far from Sol's back. They wavered and the edges smudged like they weren't quite there. She blinked and the hallucination cleared.

"They'll start growing back now that I'm here," Sol said, catching on to what she was thinking. "But it'll take forever and I don't have that kind of time. I'll have to buy some magic from the Elves."

"Elves." Jordan repeated numbly. "Of course there are Elves here." She blinked. "I think I have to lie down." She lowered herself onto the grass and put a hand over her eyes.

Sol sat patiently, turning the spit as Jordan rested. Her body was still on the outside, but a hurricane on the inside, Jordan felt like the world was spinning out of control and she was hanging on by her fingertips. She lay there until she saw stars coming out through the break in the canopy over their heads.

"How do I get home?" Jordan meant to say, but it came out as a croak. She cleared her throat and repeated the question.

"It's a problem," Sol admitted blandly.

Jordan could hear the unspoken words after it. It wasn't *his* problem.

Juices oozed from the joints of the crab claw and sizzled in the fire. The smell of cooking meat began to fill the air.

Jordan sat up and looked at the giant claw, her mouth watering with anticipation now. "How could that thing smell so bad while it was raw and smell so delicious now?" Her stomach gave a long gurgling growl.

Sol gave a half-smile. "In some places, those crabs are worth a lot of coin; the babies, anyway. The adults taste like old leather."

"You've tasted an adult?" She thought again about how big they must be and wondered how he'd managed to best one.

"Once. Never again," Sol said, taking one of his small knives and hooking it under the edge of the shell to inspect the meat. He broke away part of the shell. More juices dripped from the claw and evaporated into the flames with a hissing sound.

Jordan shoved the seemingly insurmountable problem of getting home to the back of her mind for the moment. It helped that Sol was so calm. She felt a seed of hope rooting inside her; a hope that he knew how to help her and he just wasn't saying so yet. Maybe he was just giving her an opportunity to orient herself, take a breather.

Another thought struck Jordan as she watched the smoke drift from their campfire up through the leaves. "Harpies aren't attracted to fire?"

"They might be, but we're far from the feroth carcass now and there's a lot of food there. They won't go after live prey when there's a bunch of rotting meat free for the taking."

Jordan's eyes darted around at the blackness of the forest, which now felt rather close around them. "And are there other things that might be attracted to fire? Other things with fangs or giant claws?"

"Why don't you let me worry about that?" Sol suggested. He used his knife to cut away a piece of the crabmeat and skewer it through. He handed the knife to Jordan.

She took it and sniffed the offering, her mouth watering profusely. She took a bite and almost groaned at the deliciously sweet flavor. The meat melted in her mouth like hot butter. Copying Sol, she used the small throwing knife to lift away pieces of now brittle shell and remove morsels of meat. She ate until she couldn't eat any more. Crab juice glistened on her face and ran down her hands and wrists. She got up and went back to the spring to wash.

Sol took his turn at the spring when she returned and then sat by the fire. "You'd better get some sleep. I don't know where we came out, or how far we are from a town or city. We might have a lot of walking to do tomorrow." His eyes darted to her bare feet for a second before gazing into the fire.

Jordan hid the dismay rising up inside her and fought back a wave of emotion. The fact that she now had a full belly might be the only thing standing between her and tears.

Where the hell am I? Who is this man that I have no choice but to depend on? How am I going to get home? When she thought of Allan coming home to an empty house, her eyes began to tingle.

"I don't suppose there is some way to send a message to my father from here?" Jordan asked, hopefully.

Sol huffed a laugh without a smile to accompany it and shook his head. "I don't have that kind of magic."

She gave a great exhausted sigh and lay down on her side facing the fire. "What about you?"

"I'll stay awake."

"All night?"

"Wouldn't be the first time."

"I can take a shift," Jordan offered.

Sol didn't answer.

"What? Don't trust me?"

"Should I? Everything has gone wrong from the moment I met you," Sol replied.

"In case you hadn't noticed, this situation royally sucks for me, too." Jordan crooked an elbow under her head. "If you hadn't stolen the locket from me, this wouldn't have happened."

"If you hadn't been messing with it in the first place, this wouldn't have happened," Sol's voice rose a notch. "You could have killed us both."

"I didn't know the locket was some kind of turnstile into an alternate universe," Jordan snapped, propping the heel of her hand on the dirt and sitting halfway up. She glared at Sol. "Believe me, if I had known it would bring an arrogant jerk like you into my life-" Jordan stopped talking and her face went ghostly pale. "Turnstile into an alternate universe…" she whispered, her eyes losing focus on Sol's face and drifting to the fire.

Her mother had disappeared without a trace, the back door

open, her car in the garage and clothes folded neatly in drawers and hanging color-coded in her closet. Jordan sat all the way up and put her fingertips to her temples. "I can't believe I'm only seeing it now."

"What, are you finished throwing insults?" Sol fed wood from the pile beside him into the flame.

"Be quiet for a second," Jordan put out a hand. "I need to think."

Sol rolled his eyes and poked at the flames.

Jordan's heart pounded hard in her chest, her mind raced through the possibility. A certainty filled her. *My mother had to have disappeared into the same portal. Where else could she have gone?* Jordan's whole body was swept with goosebumps. She looked up at Sol, her eyes bright.

Sol noted the look of hope and excitement on Jordan's face and a fist of anxiety throttled his stomach. That look meant she wanted something from him. He gave her a suspicious side-eye. "What?"

"Do you think everything happens for a reason?"

"Oh, boy." Sol passed a hand over his face.

"I do. I think you're supposed to help me find my mother."

Sol put out a hand against her burgeoning need, her idea. "Wait just a minute-"

"Why else would our two worlds have collided the way they did?" Jordan was talking fast now, unable to contain her excitement. "Listen, my mother disappeared a long time ago. No clues, no nothing." She sliced a hand through the air. "She was wearing the locket-"

"Slow down. This has nothing to do with-"

"You? Yes it does." Jordan rose into a crouch.

"What are you doing? Don't get up." The look on Jordan's face set his heart pounding. The last thing he needed was for her to put some kind of expectation on him. He had enough troubles of his own, now that he'd lost his wings.

"Don't you see?" Jordan crawled closer to him.

Sol cringed back as though the hope and optimism spilling out of her might burn him.

"My mother is here, in... what did you say this place was called?"

"Oriceran," Sol responded automatically, still leaning back away from her.

Jordan reached out, placing a hand on Sol's forearm and shuffled closer, now on her knees. "And now *I'm* here, closer to her than I've ever been. You know this place. If you weren't brought into my life to help me find my mother, then I'm a giant crab."

Sol took his arm out from under her touch. "You need to stop this, right now. I preferred it when you were hurling insults." He pointed at the earth on the other side of the fire. "Go lie down."

"But-"

"Now. I mean it. I'll even wake you up for a shift, if you want, just... please." He put a palm against her shoulder and gave her a small push, like he was afraid to touch her. "Go to sleep and stop talking like that. What do they say in English?" He made a little shooing motion with his fingers. "Go away."

Jordan sputtered a laugh. "That's a little harsh. Maybe reserve that one for when you're *really* upset." She crawled over to her side of the fire and lay on her back. "This conversation isn't over."

Sol grunted and shot her a wary look.

Jordan chewed her inner cheek, assessing him in the firelight. It was the first time she'd seen any look of fear on his face at all. A dislocated shoulder, giant nasty crabs and terrifying harpy screams in the distance were all fine, but she talking like she needed him brought on a look of abject terror.

CHAPTER 10

*J*ordan woke to a gentle shaking of her shoulder. The fire was still crackling nicely and warming her front, but her backside felt cool and damp. She sat up, yawned and rubbed her eyes, remembering again that she'd lost her glasses. She blinked up at Sol crouching over her. Dark circles ringed his eyes and his cheeks were ghostly pale.

"When should I wake you?" Jordan asked, another yawn making her jaw creak. A shiver passed through her and she turned her back to the fire to warm and dry her clothing. Her toes were cold and she wrapped her hands around them.

"I'll wake up with the sun," he said, moving back across the fire to lie down on his side.

"Okay," she rubbed her eyes again and blinked rapidly to wake herself. The forest was dark and quiet. An occasional call or chirp in the distance reminded her that she wasn't on Earth any more and would be able to place none of the creature noises here. The fire cast its light on the trunks and leaves around them, surrounding them in a flickering pocket. Jordan pulled her knees up to her stomach and wrapped her arms around her shins, shivering. She sat like that until her back was warmer and her front was cold and then she turned back to the fire to warm her hands and legs. Little spasms of shivers would course through her every so often, the confusion of cold and heat making her feel bone tired and stiff.

"Jordan," Sol said.

"You're still awake?" She looked across the fire and saw his half-closed eyes looking at her.

"How can I sleep with you moving around and shivering all night? Come sit here," he patted the ground in front of his belly. He said it matter-of-factly, without any awkwardness or subtext lacing his words.

Jordan crawled over and sat in front of his stomach where his hand had been. She sat stiff and upright, feeling awkward even though Sol clearly wasn't.

Sol watched Jordan sitting there with her back ramrod straight and his mouth twitched. *Clearly not a girl who's spent many nights roughing it.* He put a hand on her shoulder and pulled her back against his stomach, the tops of his thighs curled against her hip, encasing her in warmth.

When Jordan felt the heat of him, she relaxed, letting his bulk hold her up and his warmth seep into her. Gradually her shivering ceased and Sol drifted off to sleep.

* * *

"Morning," Jordan said, looking down at Sol as he cracked an eye open. A beam of light passed over her head, illuminating her messy blonde hair like a cloud of duckling fluff.

Sol grunted in response and his mouth twitched with a smile at her amusing state.

Early morning light shafted sideways through the canopy. The fire was nothing but ash and a few glowing coals, since Jordan had gone through the rest of the wood Sol had stacked.

Sol rolled over onto his back and stretched. He winced and

rubbed his shoulder, then got to his feet and gave a huge yawn, his eyes watering. He looked at Jordan. Her hair lay in tangles across her shoulders, her face was pale and her eyes were puffy. Sol's eyes drifted to the shadows of bruises forming on her arms and legs. *She took a real beating on that roll down the hill.* He noticed she had put the locket on and the long chain disappeared under her button-up shirt, between her breasts.

Jordan crossed her arms over her chest at his appraising look. "Told you I wouldn't fall asleep. How's your shoulder?"

Sol rotated it slowly. "A little stiff." He gave her a small reassuring smile. "I'll be fine."

They took turns washing and taking sips from the spring. Sol kicked dirt over the remains of the fire and the shell from the crab claw. He glanced down at Jordan's bare feet and looked thoughtful.

"Let's go," he said and began to walk through the trees. He listened for Jordan's footfalls behind him and then waited for her to complain. She didn't.

"Do you have any idea where we are?" Jordan asked.

"I have my suspicions." Sol brushed aside leaves and branches as they walked. Jordan watched his hand flash out and pick a handful of long skinny stalks of something that looked a bit like wheat. "I won't know for sure until we get beyond this brush and I get a view from higher up." He brought the stalks in front of him and seemed to be fiddling with them.

Jordan's heart dropped and she stifled a groan. Exhaustion gnawed at her consciousness and her weary, bruised body protested every step. But she clamped her mouth shut and put one aching foot after the other. She distracted herself by mulling over the possibility that her mother was indeed alive and was here, somewhere in this foreign universe. *But if that were the case, why would she not come back through the portal and come home to her family?*

"Is there a way I could send a message through to my dad?"

Jordan asked again, desperately, her eyes on Sol's spear quiver as it bumped and swayed against his back. "He's losing his mind right now. I can guarantee it."

"I'm sure there is," Sol said. "Magic can do a lot of things."

"Do you know how to do it?"

"Nope."

Jordan frowned. Getting information out of this guy was like pulling teeth. "Arpaks don't have magic?"

"Arpaks aren't particularly gifted with the use of magic, no. We rely on other species for what we need." Sol stopped walking and Jordan halted, too. Taking his knife from its sheath, Sol stepped through the thick foliage off their narrow trail going to a plant with thick, broad leaves. He sliced off two big leaves and brought them to Jordan. "Lift your foot." He bent over beside her.

"What are you doing?" Jordan put a hand on Sol's back to steady herself and lifted one bruised foot.

Sol put the broad leaf against her sole and wrapped her foot with it like a diaper. Jordan watched as he looped a long braid made of grass around her foot, fastening the leaf into a makeshift shoe. The leaf was tough and flexible. Amazed, Jordan watched as he repeated the process for her other foot. *So that's what he had been doing with the grasses he plucked.*

"They won't last more than a few days," said Sol. "But vicaris broadleaf is tough as leather when you first pick it." He released her foot and Jordan looked down at her new leafy green shoes.

"Thank you." She was caught off guard by his thoughtfulness. *Maybe he's not such an asshole, after all?*

"Don't thank me yet," Sol grunted, put his knife back in its sheath and kept walking. "I'm leaving you at the first town we come to. You slow me down too much."

Jordan's jaw dropped. *The asshole is back.* She caught up to him. "You're abandoning me here?" She couldn't believe what she was hearing. "But, I have no idea where I am, or how to get home!"

"I'll give you some money," Sol threw the words over his shoulder at her. "The right person will be able to help you."

"Who is 'the right person'?" Jordan cried, raking her hair back in frustration.

"I don't know, but it's not me. I don't have the magic you need."

"You're unbeliev-" She stopped when they broke out of the copse of trees and the view before her took her breath away.

Standing on the edge of a sheer drop off, they were looking out on a valley of incredible lushness and beauty. The rock of the cliffs was a light blonde color and clusters of green foliage clung in patches along the walls. The valley between the two cliffs was wide and sprinkled with quaint little houses and huts. Roads criss-crossed the valley and switchbacks climbed up steep mountainsides. Squared off patches of terrace crops had been built wherever the angle of the land allowed for it–even high up on pitches that Jordan would have considered too steep for agriculture. Small villages, clustered here and there, found purchase high up on the mountainsides and also on the valley floor, but none of them were very big. Tiny people could be seen in the valley below, tending crops, riding horses and driving wagons. It was a pastoral paradise.

"Wow," breathed Jordan. "I've never seen anything like this before." The valley extended beyond the horizon, as far as the eye could see; a violent, beautiful tear in the earth's skin, bracketed by those fertile mountainsides and cliff faces.

"So we are at The Conca," Sol said, resting his hands on his hips and scanning the valley. He chewed his cheek thoughtfully.

Jordan could imagine what he might be thinking. *If he had his wings, he could just take off and be on his way to wherever he needed to get to. I have to give him some credit,* she supposed, *for not bitching about it nonstop.*

She asked: "What's 'The Conca'?"

"You're looking at it. This divide runs for thousands of miles.

We're at the southern end, or it wouldn't look nearly so hospitable. In the north, it's a frozen gash of ice and storms."

Jordan stared at the beauty and abundance stretching out before her. Sol caught her look of awe. "Don't be fooled," he said. "Here be monsters, too." He turned away and began to hike along the cliff edge toward a section of mountain far less steep.

"Harpies?" Jordan asked, catching up to him.

Sol grunted.

* * *

By nightfall, Jordan and Sol had made it to the nearest town. It wasn't on the valley floor, but rather higher up, on a less steep mountainside. Jordan thought the town looked like something out of a storybook. Sharp rooflines, steep and with a dark purple thatch, loomed against the shadows of gardens and yards. The buildings had been erected every which way – as though the city planner was drunk, or just preferred chaos. Winding paths between the houses left barely enough space for two wagons to pass. Lanterns lit with three small flames dangled from the ends of short posts, casting circles of yellow light across narrow stone streets and dirt sidewalks. Strange shadows moved and swung across the stone and brick, like spooky puppets. Thick timbers bracing the houses and shops were held together with wooden spikes as thick as a man's arm. Soft lights illuminated the houses from within, giving the town a cozy feeling and the pleasant sound of laughter and talk wafted from open windows and through the alleys. A few people walked the streets, but aside from the curious glances and a nod here or there, they left the two dusty strangers alone. Even Jordan's denim shorts and curious leaf-shoes didn't seem to turn many heads.

They wound their way through the cluster of buildings until they came to the most brightly lit and welcoming of them all - a narrow tavern of three stories, stretching up like a medieval tower. Several illuminated windows graced the bottom two floors. A single dormer window on the top floor was dark. *Perhaps an empty room?* Jordan squinted at the swinging sign over the door and was pleasantly surprised when she was able to read it in the gloom. *So this is what life is like for those who don't need glasses.* There were strange glyphs painted on the sign that Jordan couldn't begin to identify, but there was a smaller line of English beneath that read *Nishpat's Folly*. She made a mental note for the tenth time to ask Sol why her eyesight had improved so much.

Jordan followed Sol in through the tavern door and raucous laughter and the smell of cooking meat hit her immediately. Her mouth began to water like a spring and her stomach growled so loudly she could feel it. Warmth from a corner fireplace seeped into her bones; her leaf-wrapped feet dragged across the wooden floor and her eyes drooped with exhaustion. She and Sol plopped themselves at the empty end of a long communal table. Jordan noticed Sol position himself with his back to the wall. Several pairs of eyes, distant but not unfriendly, took in the exhausted strangers.

Looking around, Jordan thought the tavern was the coolest building she'd ever been in. It didn't look entirely real, more like something made for show; somewhere you weren't actually supposed to sit in the chairs or drink from the mugs. Heavy, wooden beams and handmade furniture without any varnish or paint on it filled the place. Much of it had swirls and flourishes carved through it, throwing more odd shadows as the firelight danced. A collection of bizarre-looking animal horns hung over the wide fireplace – all of them coated with black soot, as though they might have come from some hellish dimension. Most of the patrons were men, chatting in a language Jordan couldn't have placed if her life was at stake. *So much for being a linguistics expert...* The men were dressed in simple homespun clothing. Many of the shirts were dyed a deep indigo color; Jordan noted that many of the hands clutching mugs were also stained indigo.

A buxom woman in a tight dress with indigo embroidery around the waist approached their table and said something in the same foreign tongue. She carried a huge tray balancing crude glass mugs filled with amber liquid and a few small pewter cups. The woman's eyes skimmed Jordan's denim shorts and short-sleeved button-up shirt and her lip curled with disapproval. Jordan was too tired to care about being judged; her eyes were on the cups. If there was water in the pewter, she intended to ask for a tub of it to drink and another tub of it to wash in. Dismissing Jordan, the maid turned to Sol for answers. Her eyes skimmed him as well and her expression melted appreciatively.

Sol greeted the barmaid in her own tongue, but then added a question with the word 'English' in it, nodding at Jordan.

"Aye, most do 'round here," said the girl, not sparing another glance for Jordan. "Two plates, two mugs?" she inquired and then set two of the pewter cups down on the table with a *clack*. Jordan snatched one up and guzzled it before even confirming it was water.

The maid watched Jordan drink, her upper lip slightly curled. She looked to Sol. "It's stew tonight. Take it or hunger."

Sol nodded. "Thanks. Have you also room for the night?"

Jordan glanced at him. A *room? Singular?* She had no money and no experience in this situation, so she clamped her mouth shut and hoped he wasn't expecting her to sleep in a horse trough somewhere.

The girl frowned and turned her head. "Wallen!" she bellowed. She set down two mugs in front of them, sloshing foam over the table.

"Might I have more water, please?" Jordan asked. The barmaid gave a jerky nod and walked away, her hips swaying.

Jordan sniffed at her mug: some kind of hoppy alcoholic beverage, but sweeter-smelling than beer. She took a sip. The cool, bittersweet liquid flooded her dry mouth. She groaned and took more long swallows. "Mead?" she guessed, before taking another long draught.

"Easy," Sol said quietly, before tasting it himself. "Not mead. Just some local brew."

A squat, bald-headed man with a big belly came shuffling up to their table on a pronounced limp. He was wiping his hands with a dingy towel. "Need room?" he grunted.

"If you'll allow," Sol returned politely. Jordan raised an eyebrow and wondered why Sol was being so deferential. *Why can't he be this nice to me?*

The man appraised the two of them. "You got business in Nishpat?"

"Just passing through," said Sol.

Wallen's eyes slid to Jordan, lingering on her face, then dropping to her chest and to her bare legs. "Top floor. Three coin."

Sol reached for his leather bag and Wallen held out his hand for the coins. Then he threw the towel over his shoulder and put his thick, butcher's hand flat on the table. He leaned toward Sol, one eye squinted. "We don't want no trouble. You know what guards this place, aye?"

Sol didn't take his eyes from Wallen's. "I do."

Wallen took his hand away from the table and palpated his double chin with it as he considered Sol. Then he nodded and dropped an iron key on the table. He limped his way behind the bar and disappeared through a wooden door that was crammed between a narrow stairwell and some shelves that were bursting with misshapen glass jugs.

"What guards this place?" Jordan whispered dramatically, taking another sip from her mug. Her head felt full of bees and her stomach sloshed like a washtub.

Before Sol could answer, the snarky barmaid returned with two full tin plates and plopped them down on the table. She took a tin cup of cutlery out from under her elbow and set it between them. She set a pewter jug of water down next and then set her hands on her hips and surveyed her work. With a last appreciative glance at Sol's hair and shoulders, she turned and swayed away.

The smell of something akin to stew hit Jordan's nose. The plate held a glob of dark brown, oily, lumpy stuff. "This looks like someone already ate it," said Jordan, taking another sniff and forgetting completely about her unanswered question. "But it smells amazing." She grabbed a spoon from the tin cup and took a bite. Her eyes drifted shut as the salty, rich flavor filled her mouth. "Oh my gawd..." She looked down at it and swallowed. "What is it?"

"It'll be a traditional dish of the valley. Probably some kind of game-stew made with illet," Sol said, taking a bite of his own. "Like your wild boar." It was good. He took another, larger mouthful as his stomach gave a gurgle of happiness.

The two of them ate like two half-starved castaways. Sol took long swallows from his mug between bites. Jordan's arms were beginning to feel like lead and her legs throbbed with a dull exhausted ache. Her feet were burning.

Jordan finished her meal first. Pushing her empty plate away, she propped her elbow on the table and rested her chin in her hand. Her neck bent as her body relaxed and drooped. Her vision swam in a soft, not unpleasant way. Jordan rarely drank and the effects of the alcohol on her exhausted dehydrated body rushed in on her like a sudden spring storm. She gazed at Sol: his dark hair tied away from his face, his strong, stubble-shadowed jaw.

"Yur handshom," Jordan slurred.

Sol stopped his spoon halfway to his mouth and his eyes found hers. He brought the spoon the rest of the way to his mouth and left it there. His hand snaked across the table, hooking the handle of Jordan's mug, pulling it away from her. He poured more water into her pewter cup and pushed it toward her. Then he bent his head and kept eating.

Jordan blew out a loose raspberry. "Too bad you're the abandoning type. But thanks for the shooooes." Suddenly she sat upright and began to half-laugh half-moan. She grabbed her right calf and massaged it roughly.

Sol looked up, alarmed. "What's the matter?"

"Leg cramp." Jordan clenched her teeth and flexed her foot while rubbing her calf. She massaged it until the cramp eased and then slumped back on the table, her eyes drifting shut. "Need a bath," she said on a sigh. "Smell like composht."

As Sol finished the last of his stew, Jordan's head dropped down onto her arm. Sol watched her for a moment through his own tired eyes. He rubbed the heels of his hands down his own quads in an effort to revive his tired legs. He wasn't accustomed to so much walking either.

An old man shuffled by with an indigo cap set at a jaunty angle over his still-generous gray hair. Only one eye was visible under the ragged brim of the old hat. He took a look at Jordan and gave a coughing laugh. He made some comment in the local dialect and gestured at Jordan with a purple stained hand. Sol knew enough of the language to catch the man's meaning - Sol wouldn't be getting anything good from his woman tonight.

Sol gave a tired half-smile and lifted his mug to the old timer without bothering to correct the assumption. He finished the drink, set the mug down and nudged Jordan's shoulder. Her body swayed limply but she didn't open her eyes. Sol sighed, got up and took the iron key. He pulled Jordan in toward his left shoulder and got an arm under her legs. With a grunt, he stood up, holding her. He winced at the ache in his injured shoulder. Jordan's head lolled forward and settled under his chin. He nodded to the barmaid, thanking her for the meal and headed sideways up the narrow staircase.

Up three floors he went with Jordan's dead weight, trying not to bash her head or feet against the walls or railing. At the third floor, he found a small landing and a single door. Sol let Jordan's legs down, but kept her weight with one arm while he jiggled the key in the old lock, letting them into the room.

The top floor of the tavern was an attic space with a small dormer window and vaulted ceilings. Moonlight streamed in through the dormer and cast the room in blue light and dark shadows. The air was stuffy and hot and smelled of musty straw. A double bed with a lumpy mattress filled almost the entire space from wall to wall.

Sol lay Jordan on the bed and pushed open the window, letting in the night air. Jordan mumbled and rolled over on her side. Her white fist was closed around something and Sol frowned and leaned over for a better look. The chain from the locket was hanging out from between her thumb and index finger.

She clings to it like a child clings to a doll, he thought, but he couldn't help the smile that touched his lips.

Sol lay down beside Jordan with his back to her. With the cool night air flowing over his face, he fell into an exhausted sleep.

CHAPTER 11

*J*ordan woke to the sounds of strange birdcalls and the smell of baking bread. She took a deep sniff and smiled, her eyes still closed. *Dad must be baking.* She frowned. Allan didn't bake. She opened her eyes and sat up, her hair skimming the beam overhead. She still had the leaf shoes wrapped around her feet. She put a hand to the locket and the events of the day before came rushing back. She rubbed her face in her hands and groaned, thinking of her dad. *He's probably frantic by now.*

She looked up, taking in the small, strange room and the empty space beside her on the bed. Jordan had no memory of going to sleep the night before. She put a hand in the dent on the coverlet. It was cold. Unless he'd paid for another room, Sol was long gone.

"That asshole," Jordan cried, getting to her feet; adrenalin brought her into full wakefulness. She never actually believed he was going to abandon her, even though he kept saying it. Her gut vibrated with a quivering panic and she bolted for the door and headed down the stairs. The barmaid from the night before was sweeping the floor in front of the fireplace with a straw broom, smearing streaks of soot into the hardwood. She stopped sweeping and looked up as Jordan hit the last step. Jordan's eyes flashed around the tavern, darting about in search of Sol.

"He left," the barmaid said, straightening. Something in her face looked oddly satisfied at Jordan's predicament.

"How long ago? Where?"

"Half hour." She resumed sweeping nonchalantly, a smug satisfaction apparent in her movements and in the tilt of her head. "Not so concerned about you, is he?"

A half hour? Jordan ignored the barmaid's question and went out through the front door into the sunny dusty streets. Men and women bustled in both directions, carrying goods, leading horses, chatting. Every person had some kind of indigo-colored clothing on, even if it was only a kerchief or a cap. Jordan's heart was pounding so hard she put a hand to her chest. She cast about for Sol's familiar dark hair and strange backwards leather vest.

He was nowhere to be seen.

Nausea rose swift and hot in her belly and she bent towards a bush, thinking she was going to throw up. Her mouth watered, but she didn't heave. A headache pounded in her temples and she put the heel of her hand to her forehead. "I can't believe he would do this to me," she muttered. "I can't believe it." She opened her eyes and took deep breaths, trying to focus on a big yellow blossom on the bush in front of her. She breathed in its scent. Squeezing her eyes shut, she did nothing but take deep, steadying breaths for fifteen seconds. Her mind was a storm. *I am alone.* Being lost and alone somewhere on Earth was bad enough, but she was lost and alone in an alternate universe, with no access to a phone or money. Sol had said he would at least give her some money, but he hadn't done that, let alone said goodbye. *He didn't even leave a note.*

Her panic began to build into fury. Sol had to be the worst kind of man to do this to a helpless person. She stood upright, clenching her teeth.

She staggered backward as someone slammed something soft into her stomach. "Ooooof!" She gasped up into Sol's face, her anger evaporating and relief flooding her limbs.

"You didn't leave!" Her arms involuntarily closed around the homespun fabric and pair of boots he handed her and Sol let go of the clothing he'd bought for Jordan with his king's money. She fought the urge to toss it all into the road and throw her arms around his neck.

"Get dressed," he said and turned away. "I'll meet you in the pub for breakfast."

"Yes, okay!" Jordan gleefully returned to the tavern and took the stairs up to the small attic room two at a time; her heart was still pounding, but now with relief. She tossed the clothing and boots on the bed and bent to untie the leaf shoes from her feet. She stripped off her filthy denim shorts, button-up shirt and sweat-stained bralette, leaving the locket around her neck. She took a sniff under an armpit and made a face. She'd been too tired to ask to bathe the night before. She cast her gaze around the room. "My kingdom for a soapy sponge," she said. "Aha!" There was a ceramic bowl and jug on a tiny washstand behind the door. Using the crusty, line-dried towel and caustic soap, she gave herself the fastest sponge bath ever, leaving her skin pink and raw.

She sorted through the articles Sol had bought, trying to figure out what to put on first. The cream-colored blouse with long sleeves and criss-crossing ties up the front went on first. She sniffed the stiff fabric. It smelled light and airy, also line-dried. *This might be the most luxurious thing I've ever worn.* Her mouth twitched as she pulled the blouse over her head. She had a closet full of designer clothing at home and suddenly this handmade blouse was the best thing ever. Funny how need had a way of fostering appreciation. The blouse fell to her hip bones, loose and already softening up.

Jordan grabbed the leggings next and held them up in the

light. Her eyes widened. They were made of leather and butter-soft. They had definitely belonged to some other woman before they'd come to her. They were a tan color, but had been worn in over the years to a golden yellow on the thighs and butt. She pulled them on and discovered they were a little on the short side, but otherwise fit. She tucked in the blouse and laced up the fly on the leather leggings. Next was the indigo-colored vest, also leather. Someone had embossed a flourish across the upper back and down along the placket where the two pieces laced together. Jordan pulled on the vest and threaded the leather ties through the holes, tightening it over her waist and ribs. Once cinched, it felt like it was doing a better job than her ribs of holding her insides together. She took a breath and imagined it felt a bit like a corset would. A pair of simple calf-length socks went on next. Uncertain as to whether they were supposed to go under or over the leggings, Jordan decided to leave them over. She held up the belt, fingering the leather ties that dangled from the back of it, unsure what they were for. Shrugging, she cinched it at her waist. She pulled on the indigo boots, which reached almost to her knees. She tightened the three buckles across the ankles and the two above her calves and stood up, flexing her feet. They seemed comfortable enough and were even fashionable, in a steampunk sort of way.

It took Jordan a few minutes to figure out what to do with three more pieces of indigo leatherwork. She eventually sorted out that two of them were wrist cuffs and the last one was an empty sheath that sat low over the hips. There was no weapon for the sheath, but Jordan put the belt on anyway. *Sol must have bought it for a reason. Maybe he has a weapon for me.* Jordan's stomach dipped with anxiety at the thought of having a knife of some kind strapped to her body - a knife that wasn't a prop for a Halloween costume. But the memory of oversized crab claws snapping at her made her cinch the sheath on tight.

The final article was a dark gray, wool cloak, with a huge

billowy hood. Jordan held it up and marvelled at the skill with which it had been made. Embroidery across the back in indigo thread displayed a large tree in the center, with smaller trees to the left and right of it. Curling flourishes in white thread made the wind that flowed through the branches. Jordan put the cloak on and discovered multiple secret pockets sewn into the lining. It was too hot to wear the cloak now, so she took it off.

Jordan smiled as she remembered how Sol had warmed her with his body heat when she was shivering. She closed her eyes. *Don't get attached, Jordan. He is not your friend. This is not your home.*

Jordan took her filthy clothing down to the bottom floor and tossed it into the fireplace. Sol was seated at a table, eating something from a wooden bowl. A second bowl had been set on the table across from him. Sol paused in his chewing, eyes sweeping her from head to toe with something like approval.

"This clothing is incredible," Jordan said, leaving out that the vest and belt were a little heavy and restrictive. She didn't want to seem ungrateful. "Thank you. I will pay you back for it. Somehow." She turned and picked up the ties swaying from her belt. "What are these for?"

"Roll your cloak up and you can fasten it there when it's too hot to wear it," Sol explained. "Or they can carry a bedroll. You can also tie up a bola with them."

"How clever! What's a bola?"

"A weapon. Speaking of weapons, I have one more thing for you." He took a blade from his satchel and set it on the table in front of what Jordan assumed was her breakfast. "I presume you know how to use one of these?"

Jordan sat at the table and picked up the knife. "Ah," Jordan said with exaggerated delight. "I've heard of these. A K-Nife, right?" She took the blade between her fingers, handle up. "It is some kind of a weapon, no? I bop my attacker over the head with the heavy part?" She made to use the handle like a club, pinching the blade between her fingers so she didn't cut herself.

Sol gazed at her through half-closed lids. "Eat." He set a bag of liquid on the table in front of her. "Here is a waterskin. Don't drink it all at once."

"You thought of everything," she said, putting the knife into the sheath at her hip. She took a mouthful of the gruel, letting it sit on her tongue for a moment. It tasted like oatmeal with a touch of honey. Sol was almost finished with his, so she shovelled spoonful after spoonful into her mouth, swallowing without chewing. She was so relieved he hadn't abandoned her that she didn't want him to have to do any waiting. She already felt like a huge burden.

"I have a job to do," Sol said, pushing his empty bowl to the side and lacing his fingers together on the table. "It's more important than our situation."

Jordan swallowed her oatmeal. *It's kind of him to use the word 'our'...* "You mean *my* situation?" She wolfed down another bite, feeling like she hadn't even eaten the night before.

"Yes." Sol took a breath. "I understand why you might think I can help you, but I can't."

Jordan swallowed and put her spoon down. She looked Sol steadily in the eye as he spoke. "I do understand that you are in the middle of something important." Jordan chose her words carefully. "That there is more at play here than I can possibly understand."

"Yes." Sol nodded. "I don't have the power to get you back home and I am bound to serve my king. Every moment that I am delayed could be the cause of a catastrophe in Rodania."

"Rodania?"

"My city and the Strix capital. I am a courier for our monarchy and I have been delayed for far too long. I need to get to the Elves as quickly as possible." At this, Sol's eyes darted to the barmaid behind the bar and he lowered his voice. "I need to get my wings back and finish my delivery. I have to go. Today. Right now. And I can't take you with me; you will slow me down too much."

Jordan fought the urge to smack her forehead down onto the table. She'd thought they were past this. Instead, she took a calming breath and said, "You need to get to the Elves." *Stay calm, Jordan. Think.*

Sol nodded. "Immediately. I have already been delayed too long."

"How far away are they?" Jordan's fingers began to tremble. She put her hands below the tabletop, between her knees.

"I had wanted to go to the Light Elves, since we have agreements with them already, but since we came out near The Conca, the Elves at the woods of Charra-Rae are much closer. All Elves have healing magic, as far as I know. I could be there in a day by wing, so..." He frowned as he calculated, "maybe three days' journey by foot."

"That's not so bad," said Jordan. "Could we not throw in together? Achieve both our goals at the same time? Couldn't the Elves at Charra-Rae help me, too? Wouldn't they know how to find my mother? How to get me back through a port-"

"Shhhh," Sol said, with another glance at the barmaid. She was behind the bar and had her back to them as she wiped glasses, but she had an ear cocked in their direction. "They would be your best bet," admitted Sol. "You could hitch a ride with a farmer to Campill and go on foot from there. You'll be safe in this valley until Usenno, at least; just don't take off the indigo clothing."

Jordan's heart began to pound and her mouth went dry. She wasn't absorbing his instructions – she was fighting the rising panic at the suggestion that she go on without him. She pushed away the remains of her breakfast. On Earth, Jordan was an independent woman who'd always been proud of never needing anyone. But this wasn't Earth; she'd never felt so vulnerable before, so lost. So needy. She hated the feeling. It festered in her like an infected boil.

"I do understand the urgency of your job. I won't slow you down. I promise," she said, locking her eyes with his.

"Jordan." Sol sighed. His eyes shuttered closed. He'd braced himself for this, but the sound of her voice plucked at him more deeply than he'd expected. *Maybe I should have left this morning without explaining anything. I could have left the clothing with the barmaid, or at the bedroom door—written down a few suggestions and then just slipped away like a ghost.*

"I'll push myself, I'm strong and I won't complain."

"No-"

"But, we're going to the same place," Jordan felt panic rising like the wind before a storm. "It doesn't make sense-"

"I'm so sorry." Sol got to his feet. A muscle in his jaw popped. "I really am. I am bound by duty."

Jordan darted to her feet too, hands wringing, breath catching in her throat.

"I don't even know what is at stake," Sol continued, softening his tone. "I'm not privy to the contents of what I carry, but I have taken an oath."

"Please," Jordan stepped toward him. "Please, Sol," she looked up into his ice-blue gaze. "Don't do this."

Sol put his hands on her shoulders. "This must be. I wish it could be different. I do." He hesitated, his face betraying a battle of wills. Jordan's eyes widened with hope. But he only said: "I wish you good fortune." And with that, he set a small bag of coins on the table and made for the door.

Jordan's hands flew to her face and her throat closed up. She covered her eyes and fought the urge to scream in frustration. Misery flooded her, as bitter and acrid as venom. She was the closest she had ever been to finding what happened to her mother... and yet so far. Her mind flashed to the rotting carcass of the beast she'd landed against, the sounds of the scissoring crab-claw. *Will I even survive in Oriceran on my own? What other terrifying beasts lie between here and the Elves of Charra-Rae? In which direction do they lie?*

Sol paused with the door open, glancing back over his shoulder. Jordan still stood at the table, her face in her hands. Sol ground his molars, wishing he hadn't looked back. He closed the door behind him.

CHAPTER 12

Sol strode away from *Nishpat's Folly* through the busy streets and buzzing market.

More like 'Sol's Folly,' he thought and then shook his head in an attempt to clear his mind. It didn't work. The image of Jordan's pleading, teal eyes looking up into his blew through his memory like a smoky apparition. *The way she'd stood there with her hands over her face...* Sol gave a low growl of frustration. *I don't have time for humans in distress. Not even a sweet, good-natured, beautiful human searching for her long-lost mother.* He kept walking, increasing the speed of his steps. *With distance and time, Jordan's voice will stop ringing in my ears; the image of her fingers over her eyes will fade.*

Sol barely noticed when the town melted away into the countryside and patches of agricultural land rolled across the chessboard tapestry before him.

'Please,' she had said. *'I promise I'll keep up.'*

Sol began to curse himself as he thought about all the things he never told Jordan. *Don't talk about going through portals with anyone but the Elves. Don't travel at night. Stay in The Conca until you reach Usenno, then climb out, rather than taking the road through the*

Passage of Skeel; the cankerworms there can siphon away the years of your life while you sleep.

The more he thought about it, the more agitated he grew. He had no way to track her, no way to know how her journey would turn out. *Will she ever find her mother?*

He cursed himself for leaving and then he cursed himself for caring. He kicked up dirt and dust with his toes as he walked, leaving gouges in the road. Advice was free, so why had his brain frozen up as soon as she'd said 'please'? He'd hightailed it out of there because if he'd stayed another second longer, he'd have cracked and he knew it. *But what if something happened to her?* The thought made his hands flex and clench. *But, what if the contents of the letter that I carry are a matter of life-and-death?*

Sol's head snapped up at the sound of screaming horses.

* * *

JORDAN STOOD outside *Nishpat's Folly* for a full ten minutes, having no idea what to do next. She chewed her lip while going over the things Sol had said to her. *Three days' journey to Charra-Rae. Best to see if I can hitch a ride to Usenno and climb out on foot from there...*

He's an ass for leaving me, but dwelling on it isn't going to do me any good. I need to mobilize. She put her back to the road they'd come in on and walked deeper into the village of Nishpat. She'd tucked the bag of coins into one of the secret pockets of her cloak, then rolled it up and tied it to her lower back with the leather straps dangling from her belt.

Merchant tables sprang up in the shade of various nooks and corners. Birdsong filled the air while the morning sun beamed down from a cloudless sky. Women and men working tables stocked with merchandise nodded politely to Jordan and held out wares for her to view: clothing, pottery, spices and tools Jordan couldn't identify. Back on Earth, Jordan had enough money to buy the entire village, but here, she had only a few coins. *It's a test,* she thought. *Just how independent and resourceful am I without my nearly bottomless bank account?* Best to save her coins for food, if possible.

She approached a broad, red-cheeked woman with a nose like melted wax and a friendly look on her face.

"Excuse me, I'm wondering if you might know anyone headed to Usenno today?" Jordan asked. "I'm willing to trade labor for a ride."

The woman squinted at her. "My English, not as good," she said. "Usenno there," she pointed down The Conca stretching off endlessly into the distance.

Jordan smiled, nodded her thanks and moved along. On the edge of town, which she reached very quickly, Jordan spotted an older man lifting burlap bags filled with something heavy—grain, perhaps–onto a small wooden wagon. The wagon had a bench seat with room for two and was hitched to a speckled pony. "Hello. Do you speak English?" Jordan asked with a smile as she neared.

The man paused in his loading and crinkled his eyes at her. "Who's askin'?" He snorted back in his throat and spat a lump of something brown off to the side before bending to pick up another sack. He bared his teeth in what might have been a smile; Jordan wasn't sure. She was sure, though, that his teeth had never seen a toothbrush.

She stepped to the side to avoid the spittle as it flew by her leg and splatted on the ground. "My name is Jordan. I'm looking for a ride to Usenno. Are you going that way?"

The man pushed the sack onto the wagon and turned back to Jordan, eyeing her more closely. "Six pieces," he grunted, bending over again. Sweat beaded on his brow and Jordan caught a whiff of sour sweat.

"Here's the thing." Jordan bent over to look into his face. "I don't have much money, but I'm strong and I can work. How about I load up the rest of this wagon for you in exchange for a ride?" There were at least two dozen more sacks to load and they looked heavy.

The man's eyes journeyed from her lips to her chest, to the chain that disappeared there between her breasts. "How about that?" He gestured.

Jordan put a hand to her chest, hiding the locket in her grip. "Oh. This isn't for trading."

"I wasn't talking about the trinket," the man said. He snorted back deep in his throat and hocked another gob onto the road. He put his hands on his hips and leered into Jordan's face, expectant.

Jordan's skin crawled and she took a step back. *This is how people barter in Oriceran?* How did he think this wasn't insulting? And why was it okay to think it was an even option?

"I'd rather walk," she said, her mouth a flat line. She turned away, but a surprisingly strong hand locked around her wrist and held her in place.

"You'll never make it on foot," he snarled, gusting rotten breath into her face. He jerked his chin toward the market behind them. "Ain't no one else going to Usenno today, mark me words." He licked his cracked lips and his eyes dropped to Jordan's hips. "I'll take you and all it'll cost you is bein' soft at the nights." He reached a hand toward her waist.

Jordan's face flushed with indignation and disgust. She yanked her hand out of his grip and drove her fist into his gut. It wasn't her hardest shot, but it was enough to send a message.

"Oooof!" The man doubled over. Several faces looked their way in concern and Jordan backed away from the man. She heard someone shout in her direction and she began to walk quickly down the road, away from town. Usenno on foot it would be; or maybe she could find a ride from someone less sleazy the next town over. A different hand clamped down on her shoulder and

Jordan turned to look up into the face of a large man with a thick red beard.

"Take your hand off me, please," Jordan said through clenched teeth.

His meaty fingers squeezed, biting into her shoulder. "This the girl?"

The barmaid from *Nishpat's Folly* stepped out from behind him, her nose in the air and that smug curl in her upper lip. "Aye, that's her."

Jordan glared at the girl.

"Yer comin' with me, you are," the bearded man snarled. Another hand closed around her upper arm. "Talk of breaking the treaty will land you in Trevilsom mighty quick." He spoke slowly and nodded as though convincing himself that this was true.

"She can't be that bright," sniffed the barmaid, setting a hand on a hip. "Talking about portals where people can hear."

"I won't ask you again," Jordan seethed, ignoring the barmaid. "Remove your hand."

Allan had put Jordan into self-defense and mixed martial arts classes when Jordan was only six. She'd hated the classes and fought her father to quit; he had told her she could quit when she was sixteen and she did. Now that she had a vicelike fist around her bicep, she was grateful for her dad's deal and Jordan's mind settled into that quiet place it lived when she'd been forced to spar.

The bearded man yanked on her upper arm, turning back towards town and dragging Jordan with him. The barmaid fell into step just in front of them. She crossed her arms and raised her chin like a queen.

Jordan windmilled her arm, breaking the man's grip. Just as he turned to snatch at her, she sent the heel of her right hand into his nose. She felt a crunch as it broke. He grunted in pain as blood spurted down his chin and into his mouth, reddening his teeth. His hands flew up to his damaged face and Jordan grabbed his testicles with her left hand and squeezed. The man gave a garbled cry and froze, afraid to pull away from her, afraid to even move.

The barmaid began to scream words Jordan didn't understand, but she figured it was safe to bet that she needed to get out of Nishpat, fast. People were beginning to draw close and a loose semicircle took shape around them.

Jordan peered up into the giant's face. "I'm going to let go. And you're going to let me walk away. You got that?"

The bearded man whimpered in his throat while blood flowed freely from his broken nose. He nodded, his eyes tearing up. At least this was one thing that was the same here as it was on Earth: Bullies were cowards at heart. That and testicles meant leverage.

"If anyone comes after me, it'll be you I come for," she continued. "Next time, I'll take one of these…" She squeezed his balls until he choked and turned a shade of green. "…with me."

The barmaid had disappeared into the crowd somewhere, but Jordan could hear her yelling, gathering her forces. Jordan let go of the man's bits and strode down the road, right past the old man whom now sat on his cart holding his gut. He glared at her as she passed by. It took all she had not to break into a panicked arm-flailing sprint.

The falling of footsteps followed by the raised voices of a scuffle sounded behind her, making her glance over her shoulder. Half a dozen men were talking with the red-bearded man, who had a hand cupped over his genitals. They seemed to be having an argument and gesturing in her direction. Four of them broke into a jog after her. Jordan took off like a shot, dodging a cart and passing two riders on horseback. The horses whinnied and tossed their heads as she sped by them, her booted feet thundering on the dusty road.

As she ran, Jordan's hand drifted down to the blade Sol had

given her. She was both thankful to have it and terrified to use it. *Why didn't I sign up for weapons training all those years ago?* She was confident in self-defense against one other person; it didn't even matter if that person was bigger than her. *Against four big men?* She looked back over her shoulder. *Well, three*–it seemed she'd lost one–but they looked mad.

Jordan sprinted around another wagon and stopped short as a man on horseback, with a second horse in tow, came galloping up the road toward her. They were too close for her to dodge; their flying hooves were upon her. She dropped to a crouch and covered her head, hoping they'd go around or over her. When the hoofbeats stopped just in front of her, she looked up. Sunlight flashed brightly behind the rider's head, blocking out his face, but it didn't matter; she'd recognize Sol's silhouette anywhere.

"You came back," she cried. Dust clouded up around her from the stomping hooves and she coughed.

"Let's not go on about it," said Sol. "Can you ride?" Without waiting for a response, Sol tossed the reins of the second horse, a gray mare, to Jordan.

Jordan snatched the reins and, grinning, told him, "I love riding." Sol's dark brown horse had a saddle, but the gray one didn't–only a strange looking bosal around her nose. Jordan mounted the mare as three men from the village skidded to a halt in the road.

One of them yelled, sending spittle flying. He was addressing Sol, but pointing at Jordan.

Sol looked over the heads of the men towards the small crowd of peasants, farmers and merchants who were now gathered at the edge of town, watching. He caught a glimpse of a big, red-bearded man with dark blood clotting on his chin and in his beard. He was massaging his genitals with one hand, as though ensuring they were intact. The barmaid from *Nishpat's Folly* hooked a hand under Red-Beard's elbow, but he yanked his arm away. He turned his back to the barmaid and disappeared into the crowd.

Sol ignored the yelling townsmen, wheeled his horse around and took off down the road at a gallop. Jordan followed on her gray, kicking up dust behind them.

CHAPTER 13

"Where did you get the horses?" Jordan asked, patting the mare's neck once they'd slowed to a walk, matching each other stride for stride.

"I relieved their former owner of them," Sol said, jaw tight. "Some people shouldn't own animals." The gelding gave a blowing snort as though he agreed.

Jordan's eyes skimmed the legs of the horse under Sol. A cloth bandage had been wrapped around the ankle joints of both front legs. She frowned and leaned over enough to peer down at her own horse's legs. The same kind of wrapping had been administered to her gray. "They were hobbled?"

Sol gave a nod. "With chains."

Jordan's face heated with anger. "Are you sure they're okay to ride?"

"They are now. I put a nyopsis poultice on them. The stuff fills every ditch in this place."

"It's a healing herb?"

"It's a magic herb," explained Sol. "It'll close up their wounds and numb any pain. I'll have to apply more tomorrow."

Jordan nodded, making a mental note to learn what this

amazing herb looked like. "Do you think they'll come after us?" Jordan asked glancing at the road behind them.

"Doubt it. Any reward they might get for turning you in wouldn't be worth the trouble."

"Turning me in for what? And to who?" The barmaid had admonished her for talking about portals, but surely talk wasn't enough to condemn someone.

"Maybe to a local magistrate who has a connection to an enforcer," Sol shrugged. "Going through portals is illegal. Happens anyway and getting away with it isn't very hard if you know the right people. But, every once in a while, someone has to go to prison for it."

"You said it was dangerous," Jordan reminded him. "That people can be killed that way."

Sol was quiet as they passed a woman on horseback going towards Nishpat. She had huge saddlebags packed with metal goods that rattled with an endless cacophony. The woman grimaced at them apologetically as she passed. The clanking was sharp enough to make Jordan wince.

Sol waited until the woman and her metal clatter was far enough behind them that he could be heard before he answered. "They can and are. Passing through portals can be risky business."

"We seemed to manage it okay."

"We were lucky," Sol said. "I don't know where that locket came from, or how it got charged up with magic, but we are very lucky it had enough power in it to take us both through all the way. You remember those whispering voices you heard on the way through?"

Jordan nodded grimly, remembering.

"Those were the ones caught in-between. Now that the locket is back in Oriceran, it'll charge up again. But while it was on Earth, it would have slowly drained of power. That's when it's at its most dangerous."

"So, it should be able to take me back?"

Sol shrugged. "Maybe yes, maybe no. Like I said, it's not very sophisticated."

"Could the Elves tell me?"

"Probably."

Jordan was satisfied with this for now. It seemed like her whole life was hinged on getting to the Elves of Charra-Rae. She and Sol fell into a companionable silence for a time as they rode over hill and dale. They passed endless picturesque farmland.

The sun was reaching its peak and Jordan found herself wishing for sunglasses. All the squinting was beginning to give her a headache.

Sol retrieved a lump of something black from his satchel. He steered his gelding closer to Jordan and handed it to her. "Put this under your eyes. It'll help with the glare."

"Like a football player!" Jordan took the kohl, delighted. She did her best to smudge the kohl neatly under her bottom lids. "This okay?"

"Perfect." Sol tried not to grin at the uneven smudges under her eyes and took the kohl back.

"How do you know all this stuff?" Jordan straightened and dusted off her hands. "You knew how to speak whatever language it is these valley people speak. You knew where we were as soon as you saw The Conca. You know that my locket only has," she made air quotes with her fingers, "'rudimentary magic'. You even know my shoe size."

"I'm an Arpak courier," Sol answered, as though that should be enough.

"Do they teach you how to explain yourself to an Earthling in courier school?"

Sol cracked a grin, showing the dimples in both cheeks.

"Sweet jaysus on a pony," Jordan said. "He does smile."

"Actually, they do," Sol said, relaxing. The sound of the horses' hooves against the hard-packed dirt road was comforting. Birds twittered and scuds of clouds moved slowly across a blue sky.

The day was warm and Jordan felt her cheeks absorbing the sun's rays. At this rate, her face would be brown as a nut in a few days. She wondered if Oriceran's sun was any different from Earth's.

"Arpak couriers are among the most broadly educated of Rodania's citizens," Sol stated matter-of-factly. "We aren't specialists in the way a doctor or a lawyer is; we're more like a jack-of-all-trades."

"Good at a little bit of everything." Jordan nodded.

"Except geography. We're *great* at geography," Sol said, nudging his gelding around a pothole filled with rocks. "Couriers are made to memorize the geography of Oriceran."

"How big is Oriceran?"

Sol raised his eyebrows and a dimple appeared in one cheek. "Bigger than your Earth."

"What?" Jordan's jaw dropped. The idea of memorizing the geography of America was daunting enough. "How can you memorize that much territory?"

"They break it down into zones over four years of University. We have more water than you, but we still have a lot of land. We start with the local zones, as they're most important. And after we pass the test for that zone, we move outwards in concentric circles."

"Place names *and* terrain?"

"Yes, as well as local dialects, vegetation, animal inhabitants, any magical predilection, history all the way back to before the Great War, local militant groups, if there are any, treaties, established trade routes, cultural norms," Sol's voice was beginning to drone. "Magical species, inventions-"

"Inventions?"

"Political leanings, prejudices and minority groups..."

"Holy moly."

"Local slang, religions, the evolution of warfare in the area..."

Jordan was staring at Sol like he'd sprouted another head.

"Negotiation techniques, economics, architectural styles and practices..."

"Stop, stop, stop." Jordan put a hand out. "What!" *Jack-of-all-trades' is right. How can anyone retain that kind of information?*

"That doesn't include what we have to learn about Earth," Sol added with a smile.

"You have to study Earth, too? You should run for president," Jordan joked. "Our presidents seem to be great at lying and schmoozing these last few years, but not much else. We could do with an insanely overeducated, flying bird-man to shake things up."

"We don't have presidents," continued Sol as the horses slowed for a steep downhill descent.

Getting an idea, Jordan held onto her horse with her thighs to free her hands and untied the cloak. She shook it out and folded it in half. The mare skittered to the side and Jordan's left knee bumped against Sol's calf. "Sorry," she said. She lifted herself up by bracing against the mare's withers and pushed part of the cloak under her butt.

"What are you doing?" Sol reached a hand out to steady her by the shoulder.

"Just trying to make a bit of a saddle to protect the mare's spine."

"Oh." He was watching Jordan, who had managed to stay on a rocking bare back, going downhill, while tucking the folded cloak beneath her. She had most definitely ridden before. Sol's face warmed at the thought that frolicked through his brain following that one. He blinked and looked away from Jordan's thighs.

"What's the matter?" Jordan settled herself again.

"Nothing. Why?"

"Your face is all pink."

"It's hot out." Sol made a show of casting his gaze over the crops on their left.

"Sure is," said Jordan. She looked down at the leather vest encasing her torso and found herself wishing she could take it off. "So, if I were to ask you who Abraham Lincoln was-"

"An American president," said Sol, without hesitation. "One of your more beloved ones, I think. I couldn't tell you which number he was exactly, but I'd hazard somewhere around fifteen or sixteen. He was assassinated in a theater, right?"

"Bang on," Jordan said, then caught herself. "No pun intended. How about Nikola Tesla, do you recognize that name?"

Sol squeezed an eye shut. "An... inventor? I think."

"Wow." Jordan was genuinely impressed. "Do you speak any French?"

"Quel plaisir de faire ta connaissance, mademoiselle," said Sol with a near perfect accent.

"You're scary."

Sol laughed and waggled his eyebrows in the first real playful expression he'd ever made. "You should see me with wings."

Jordan smiled. "I can't even imagine it." She liked this new, relaxed Sol; now that he'd made the decision to allow her to come with him, he was a lot less of an asshole.

"It doesn't seem fair," she said, gazing off at the rolling green horizon that disappeared between the blonde cliff walls in the distance.

"What?"

"You know everything about us and we know nothing about you."

"Some Earthlings know," said Sol. "And I am a far cry from knowing everything. What I have is theoretical knowledge, taught from history books brought through a portal illegally."

But Jordan's mind caught on the first thing he said. "Which Earthlings know about Oriceran?"

Sol shrugged. "Whoever might benefit the most from trade with us. We have a saying in Rodania: 'Follow the magic'. I would imagine your elite families and higher-up politicians would know about it."

"Huh." Jordan went quiet. The saying on Earth was to 'Follow the money,' but she supposed magic might even be more valuable than money to some. *Wouldn't it be nearly impossible to keep something like an alternate universe full of magic a secret?*

Her mom was more than likely here. Jordan felt sure of it. *So why had Jaclyn never told Allan about it?* Jordan's skin prickled. *Or does he know about it, too and is keeping it from me to protect me?* Her dad was a politician. Not super high up, but a state senator was nothing to sneeze at.

"How many portals are there?" Jordan asked.

"Oh, I have no idea," Sol shook his head. "I don't know if anyone knows that. I suppose someone might be trying to map them, but it wouldn't be easy. New portals could be made and old ones could be sealed off." He shrugged. "I couldn't even begin to guess."

"You didn't study portal geography in school?"

"Not in such detail. Arpak couriers don't ever need to leave Oriceran."

"What if someone wants to deliver a letter to someone on Earth?"

"They wouldn't get an Arpak to do it," Sol answered dryly with a jerk of his thumb towards the slashes in the back of his vest. "Look what happens to us when we pass through a portal."

"Why does that happen?"

"Same reason that makes your locket dangerous: our wings are magical," said Sol. "Magic fades on Earth."

"But your wings didn't just fade," pointed out Jordan.

"No, they didn't." Sol remembered the sickening pain and then the blackness after he'd hit the tree. "Gone in a second, but they'll take years to grow back."

"*Years?*"

Sol nodded.

"How come you can't just magic them back yourself?" Jordan asked, swirling her fingers over her shoulder as though trying to conjure her own wings.

"As I said, Arpaks aren't particularly good with magic."

Jordan bent her head to peer at his face. "You sound unhappy about that."

"Well, it would be nice not to make a deal with a damn Elf every time we needed something," he grumped. "Arrogant sods."

The descent flattened and a cloud moved across the sun, casting them in shadow. Jordan closed her eyes as a cool breeze blew across her damp forehead. She looked straight down the valley and ahead of them. Jordan marvelled at how well she could pick out the moving creatures on the vista before her. "Do you have any idea why my eyesight is so much better here on Oriceran than it is on Earth?"

Sol blinked at her. "Your eyesight is better here?"

"Way better," said Jordan with emphasis. "I need pretty strong glasses or contact lenses just to get around normally. Doesn't seem to be the case here. I can even see all the men and women working in the crops down there, even though they're little."

Sol frowned and followed her gaze. "I don't know why. That's strange."

The two of them mused separately about this as the rhythmic hoofbeats of their horses carried them deeper into the gorge.

* * *

WHEN THE SUN DESCENDED, withdrawing its light and warmth from the valley, Sol negotiated a patch of grass in a farmer's yard for them to sleep on. The farmer, a jovial man who spoke no English, gave them firewood for the pit in his yard and buckets of grain for the horses. He even welcomed them to the water troughs that his own animals drank from; though Sol offered extra money for food, the farmer held up a hand and shook his head.

After Sol and Jordan had settled themselves in front of a fire for the night, the farmer's portly wife came waddling across the grass carrying two steaming bowls. She bobbed her head as Sol thanked her and waddled back inside their little thatched cottage.

"They are very sweet," said Jordan around a mouthful of stew. It seemed to be the flagship dish of The Conca.

"Most of the people in The Conca are," agreed Sol. "They just want to be neighborly and live a good, simple life."

They filled their bellies with the warm food and Jordan delivered the dishes back to the house after rinsing them in the trough. She wrapped herself up in her cloak and hunkered down by the fire. Things always looked better with food in the stomach and a fire to cozy up to. Her eyes flicked to Sol, who sat cross-legged with his elbows on his knees and his chin in his hands. He had no jacket to cover his arms, nor a cloak.

"Will you be cold?" Jordan asked, lifting the corner of her cloak, offering to share.

Sol shook his head. "I'll be fine."

Jordan nodded, but found herself feeling disappointed. *That's interesting,* she thought as her chin drifted onto her chest.

It seemed she'd only just closed her eyes when Sol was jiggling her shoulder to wake her. The sun was a mere suggestion on the horizon as Sol saddled his horse and Jordan fixed the bosal and cloak onto the mare. They splashed their faces in the trough and refilled their waterskins. They were back on the road, rubbing sleep from their eyes and yawning widely enough to crack their jaws, before the lights were on in the farmer's cottage.

Sol produced an apple and handed it to Jordan silently. She took it, but felt too sleepy to eat. The horses plodded on into the still-deep shadows of early morning.

CHAPTER 14

Noontime found Sol and Jordan entering new terrain. Farmers' huts and fields of crops grew sparse and the towns dwindled to nothing. The horses carried the travelers deeper into wilder, drier territory. The cliff walls narrowed. Sunlight shifted and danced across the cavern walls and a brisk wind drove the clouds across the sky. Deep shadows congealed beneath overhanging crags.

Much more awake now, Jordan admired the primeval beauty of the chasm, no doubt a savage product of titanic violence. "Sol," she began. "Do you know when-" A rancid smell swept over her as the wind changed and her hand flew to cover her nose. Both horses tossed their heads and the gray let loose a chilling whinny. "What is that?" Jordan gagged as another gust of wind struck her full in the face with that sickly smell—a putrid combination of sour sweat and rotting meat.

Sol's eyes darted upward, across the cliff walls and then locked onto a patch of darkness as it detached itself from the underside of a crag. The shape coalesced into a vast winged form, silhouetted against the sky; it was small in the distance, but rapidly growing. Dread settled deep in the pit of Sol's stomach.

"Harpy!" Sol snapped the word out. "Jordan, to the trees. Make for the trees! And *stay there*. Don't you dare come out!" The words were a barked command and Jordan barely recognized Sol's voice. His deadly serious tone brought gooseflesh out on her arms. The winged shape drifted down upon them with slow, almost lazy strokes. There was only time for a fleeting impression of greasy black feathers, tattered leathery wings—with a span Jordan couldn't comprehend—and a massive head of wrinkled, scabby skin topped by great horns. It wasn't until Sol shouted her name a second time that she threw off her paralyzing fright and put her heels to her horse. The mare dug her hooves into the dirt, her haunches flexing with power as they bolted forward.

Jordan crouched like a jockey, her head low against the mare's neck. She clamped down hard with her thighs as the horse bolted for the bush. A copse of trees–slim-trunked but with many interwoven branches–drew closer with what seemed like horrifying slowness. The wind ripped at her hair as they galloped.

A dark shape streaked past. It was close enough for her to reach out and touch, but she wasn't that stupid. Sol's horse, now riderless, surged ahead of Jordan and the mare. Clumps of dirt and sand flew into Jordan's face. She peered back over her shoulder, fear tightening her windpipe as she prepared to halt. She thought Sol had been thrown, but no, Sol stood upon the road, dust still settling around his planted boots. He held a lightweight throwing spear in his right hand and the blade from his belt in the left. He'd discarded his two satchels in some unseen place, leaving his shoulders unencumbered.

The sight of him made Jordan's blood run cold. *He's planning to fight that monstrous thing?* Jordan watched in horror as Sol clanged the blade of his sword with the head of his spear, the sound of steel clashing on steel ringing through the canyon. The stench of rotting meat grew stronger. Jordan's eyes darted up to the harpy, whose trajectory seemed bound directly for her and the horses.

"*Ela stohn, daemona!*" Sol bellowed foreign words at the oncoming monster. "Over here, you old hag-crow!" Jordan's skin crawled. This was altogether a different Sol. There was a screeching cry from the beast, almost as though she'd understood him and she redirected; diving instead for the lone man standing in the path between the two cliff faces.

Jordan's heart swelled with a strange cocktail of outrage, fear and gratitude. Hauling back on the reins as they finally broke into the trees, she battled both her own terror and that of her horse. The gray seemed intent on carrying her straight through the close-knit trunks, all the way to the cavern wall. "It's alright." Jordan murmured sweet lies to the gray, keeping her voice calm with great effort as she slowed the animal. Jordan's heart pounded in her ears and her mouth was dry with fear. *Keep it together.* If she showed her terror, she would lose control of the horse completely. Jordan spied Sol's gelding just beneath the canopy; it appeared to feel safe enough within the trees, but was unwilling to go further without his companion. He tossed his head and whinnied.

They joined the dark horse and Jordan leapt from her mare's back. Grasping the reins of both, she lashed them up, out of harm's way. Skipping around their dancing hooves, Jordan turned back to the unfolding scene on the road. Her heart leapt into her throat as the harpy swooped down on Sol with a ragged cry.

Sol took a series of rapid steps forward to meet the harpy, his arm and head canting back and he hurled the short spear. The missile flew straight and true, passing through light and shade, reflecting glints of sunlight from the metal head. The spear should have taken the harpy straight between the eyes, but with frightful intuition, the harpy bucked her head downward and the spearhead rattled, leaving a gouge upon her scalp below the right horn. The harpy's scream became a croak of pain and she fought to keep herself in the air as her head thrashed, slinging thin trails of purple-black blood.

That simple but intelligent, evasive move on the harpy's part struck a cold hard fear into Jordan's heart, as sharp as an arrow. This was no mindless predator. The beast was *canny. This harpy is female. I don't know how I know, but I do.* Jordan could feel, without a doubt, that the monster Sol was facing was a terrifying old matriarch. Perhaps it was the puffy breast jutting proudly outward, or the elegant curve of her horns. The scars crisscrossing her skull and wattle told of many battles-battles she hadn't lost.

The monster's talons sailed harmlessly over Sol's head. Sol stood his ground as he watched her swoop upward and take a banking turn. His sword was now in his right hand, his left having drawn a leaf-bladed throwing knife.

Back the demon came, her talons reaching out, bloody horns pinned back against her neck. Sol's throwing knife flashed and was buried to the hilt somewhere in her torso–but with no discernible effect. It was a hornet's sting against a creature more than twice Sol's height. Soundlessly, the beast was on him.

Jordan screamed as the harpy's talons flashed downward and the wattled head shook with effort, but Sol darted nimbly to the side. Light as a dancer, he leapt to thrust his sword at her lowered head and gaping maw. Silver steel tore through a flap of hanging flesh under her chin, spilling more rank blood. The pierced flesh, flaccid and dragging, tore the sword from Sol's grip as she barrelled past overhead and Sol's shoulders and back flexed in an odd manner just before the harpy's sweeping wing knocked him to the ground, hard. The harpy landed in the dirt on strong, splayed talons and turned her monstrous form. Jordan got the impression of a heavy warship making a turn in the sea—swinging deadly guns to face its target.

"Sol!" Jordan screamed. She pulled the knife from the belt at her hips, looking down at what now seemed a puny and useless defense. Sol's words rang in her memory. *'Don't you dare come out!'* She looked up, eyes wide as she watched Sol do battle. From her vantage point, he looked like a small man under a monster made of nightmares.

Sol rolled about on the road, kicking up dust as the harpy snapped down at him with its short, dragon-like jaws, a deadly hooked beak at the tip. She waddled and bounced about, far clumsier on the ground than in the air. Her feathers produced a fetid wind. Each time Sol seemed to make it clear enough to stand, she would hop into the air with a flap and come crashing down with scoring talons. Sol rolled aside and the deadly game would repeat itself.

A thick, warbling sound bubbled out of the fiend's fleshy throat. *The harpy sounds like she is enjoying herself,* Jordan thought. *Like a cat toying with a mouse.* The harpy knew her prey would tire soon; then it would be so easy to drive one of those twelve-inch talons home, or rip at him with her beak.

With monumental effort, Sol finally sprang clear. He landed in a crouch with twin daggers in his fists, the weapons straight and needle-sharp. As the monster came down, Sol jumped straight up. The harpy's talons snapped together in the air just under him. He slammed both daggers into the feathers above her scaly legs.

The harpy screeched and Sol felt the hot blood gout over his hands and forearms. Like a mountain climber driving spikes into rock, Sol began to climb the harpy's body using his daggers. Jordan could only imagine the agony his injured shoulder would be in, but he climbed like he didn't feel any pain. The harpy writhed and flailed, her wings beating the air frantically as the metal spikes dug into her flesh.

With blood coating his arms up to his shoulders, Sol's hands slipped from his knives and he crashed back to the earth, landing hard on his back. With a wild leap, the harpy twisted and hooked a stabbing talon into Sol's shoulder, piercing the leather of his vest. She gave a powerful flap, lifting him into the air, and with a hateful flick, she threw Sol back to the ground. This time he landed on his stomach–all the air knocked out of him in an audible *whoosh*. The harpy did not give him a chance to recover. The talons scythed out again, this time finding the openings where his wings should have been. Sol spasmed soundlessly on the ground.

A scream tore from Jordan's throat. The harpy loosed her own pained wail as she floundered backward, her beak snapping down at her belly. The hilts of Sol's daggers still glittered in the creature's feathered flesh.

As the harpy fell away, ripping at her own feathers to tear loose the metal spines, Jordan snatched her cloak from the mare's back and made a run for Sol. Sliding in the dirt, Jordan saw close up what she couldn't see from afar. Blood welled from the slashes in Sol's leather, his torn flesh wet and red underneath. He was unconscious but breathing. She struggled to keep her gorge down. *So much blood*. Her hands worked to tear a strip from her cloak. "Hold on, Sol. We'll get you to the trees," she panted. How she was going to execute this directive evaded her. *There's no way I can carry him.*

A dark shadow fell across them, followed by the sound of metal pinging off stone as Sol's knives landed in the dirt nearby. Jordan looked up. The corners of the harpy's mouth seemed to twist in a grin as she cocked her head to one side. The intelligence Jordan saw in her crimson eyes turned her blood to ice. *This is it. We're toast. Death by harpy.* Jordan's heart gave a painful squeeze for her father. *He'll never know what became of me.* Jordan refused to look away as the harpy opened her beak and drew her head back to strike. Jordan grasped the hilt of her knife, her knuckles white, preparing to slash out.

A strange whirring missile buzzed through the air and with a sharp *crack*, one of the harpy's horns fell to the ground—alongside an axe with a broad blade and a short, curved handle. Croaking in dismayed rage, the harpy craned her neck, casting about for her new enemy.

Jordan worked frantically in the extra moments she was given, putting pressure on Sol's wound and wrapping strips of fabric over his shoulder and under his arm. She looked up in short bursts to see another winged form descending, hugging the cliff walls as it came. Immense bat-like wings spread from the broad, muscled back of a man bedecked in dark leather. Her eyes widened. *Is this what Sol looks like when he has his wings?*

Jordan pressed down on Sol's wounds and he gave a piteous groan. His face was as pale as paraffin. Leaving one hand on the bandages, Jordan used her free hand and her teeth to tear more strips of cloth from her cloak to pack the wound. She wanted to believe that the bleeding had slowed down, but the way the fabric was turning dark wasn't a good sign.

Kicking up more nauseous wind, the harpy took to the air, rising to meet the new figure as he skimmed along the canyon wall, his booted feet running sideways along the stone. The bat-winged man pushed off into a dive. With frantic wing strokes, the harpy made to match his speed and meet him in the air. The collision of the two flyers was imminent and it seemed the harpy would crush the man into the canyon wall.

Jordan held her breath, expecting to see the stranger swiftly destroyed. At the last second, though, he barrel rolled and then flared his wings, banking hard away from the cliff. Unable to turn so quickly, the harpy smashed into the canyon wall with an impact that made Jordan's teeth rattle. Dazed, the beast plummeted to the canyon floor in a jumble of wings and feathers.

The man climbed higher, catching updrafts and vaulting nimbly upward. The harpy raised her head, glaring with concussion-bleared eyes as the warrior drew two wide-bladed knives from the harness around his torso. Steel glittered in his hands—a cold promise reflecting in the patchwork light. The harpy gave a hoarse screech as it swung about looking for its attacker. She gathered herself for a leap, but the warrior hurled his knives with a flick of the wrist, one following the other in quick succession. The blades spun and patches of feathers fell from her; her black body was slick and wet with blood. The creature's enraged cry filled the air and she spread her wings and began to climb. Both creatures worked to gain altitude. The harpy's wings flapped laboriously in comparison to the man's easy, powerful strokes.

Enraged, the harpy tried to use its bulk to crush the man sideways into the jagged cliffside. The warrior tucked his wings tight to his body and took hold of a rock spur jutting from the canyon face. Spinning around the spike of stone, he launched himself up and to the side so he landed upon the cliff face, clinging there like a spider. The hooks at the tops of his wings latched onto the rock, stretching his wings wide; from the back, he really did look like an overgrown bat. The harpy had to wheel away from the wall and swing around in a wide circle to avoid crashing into the wall herself.

The warrior did not stay in his position long, but launched himself higher and the harpy followed in hot pursuit. Soon they were in the much more open upper levels of The Conca, seeming almost to touch the sun-punctured clouds.

Down on the canyon floor, Jordan squinted up at the battle that held their lives in the balance.

With a surge of effort, the man put more distance between himself and the pursuing monster. At the height of his climb, he drew a short spear from the sleeve between his wings and threw it straight up into the air, beating his wings furiously to follow it.

"She's below you," murmured Jordan in dismay. "Wrong way, genius."

But the spear slowed, paused and then turned, gravity drawing the heavy iron head downward. The winged man gave an elegant, almost lazy spiral, meeting the spear shaft in the air with his hand and sending it straight down at the enemy with terrifying speed and precision.

"Oh," Jordan whispered, understanding. Her forearms prickled at the power of the throw and the practiced skill that had launched it.

The harpy gave a shrill cry of fear and tried to change directions. All her struggling managed to accomplish was opening her chest wide to the driving spear tip. The head drove clean through the harpy's muscular breast, piercing her laboring heart.

Jordan stopped breathing as the two creatures seemed to hang still in the sky. The moment of death and defeat for the harpy and magnificent victory for the winged warrior, would be forever seared across her memory. She'd never forget the visual of that breadth of time. She also understood in one swift moment why artists painted and poets wrote of battle.

Then the harpy's great heavy carcass fell from the sky as though she had turned to stone. The man descended casually after his foe's corpse, drifting like a feather.

Jordan felt, as much as saw, the harpy crash to the ground; the impact resulting in a cringe-inducing crunch. For several heartbeats, she stared at the monster's corpse, certain that, even after all the fighting and all her wounds, the horrid creature might still rise up. Then the winged man landed upon her broken body and pulled his spear free with a sharp yank. Jordan breathed a sigh of relief and turned her attention back to Sol.

A gust of air blew strands of Jordan's sweat-soaked hair from her face as booted feet landed in the dirt a short distance away. Hands keeping pressure on Sol's wounds, Jordan looked up into the face of their rescuer.

CHAPTER 15

He was tall and long-legged, long-armed and long-fingered. He stood with a tense energy, seeming ready to explode into action at any second. His pale face was lined with brutal experience and seamed with old scars, but his gray eyes were keen and cool. His beard and hair were silver, trimmed short and neat. Dark leather armor, not unlike Sol's, encased his chest; the only exposed flesh was on his pale, sinew-knotted arms. Leather bracers protected his forearms from wrist to elbow and were dyed the same striking indigo as Jordan's vest. The winged man spoke to her in a foreign tongue and Jordan recognized the words as sounding similar to the dialect she'd heard from the people in Nishpat.

"Do you speak English?" she asked, her voice hoarse. She coughed to clear it. Her pulse was still thrumming like mad. Jordan released one hand from Sol's back to wipe her hair from her eyes and the sweat from her brow. Sol lay with a terrifying stillness beneath her pressing hand.

The man looked surprised. "Since when do girls from The Conca prefer to speak English?" His accent was strange but not unpleasant. His voice was deep and seemed to rumble from his chest like a rolling boulder. He rolled his 'r's, which made Jordan think of a Scottish brogue.

"I'm not from The Conca," Jordan answered. She covered her nose as the stench of the dead harpy drifted toward her on the breeze. Her eyes watered.

The man wiped the harpy blood from his blades on tufts of grass, then produced a rag from his pocket and cleaned off the rest. "No? You're wearing the color."

"Sol bought me some clothes in Nishpat." Jordan looked down at Sol and the bandages around his torso dark with blood. "This is Sol." Jordan swallowed hard at the ashen color of her companion's face.

"And you?" The stranger replied. "What name are you?"

"Jordan." Her body trembled and her muscles felt fatigued from being shot through with adrenalin. She held out a hand to the their rescuer. "Where I'm from, we shake hands when we make a new friend." She only realized afterward that her hand was bloody, but it was too late to withdraw it.

The man looked down like he needed a second to remember what to do with it. His expression cleared and he stepped forward and took it, seeming not to mind the blood. The skin of his palm was thick and calloused. They shook.

"Toth," he offered in return.

"Sorry about the blood," she said.

"Blood is a consequence of my job." He dismissed her apology, wiping his hand on the rag he still held. His eyes were a light gray, but bright enough to be startling. Black kohl had been applied on his bottom lid with a much more practiced hand than Jordan's. With his enormous leathery wings folded up behind him and the long black claws at the tops of his wings curving inward to make a sinister frame for his face, their defender cut a terrifying figure. With the multitude of throwing and fighting weapons strapped to his body, he gave new meaning to the phrase 'armed to the teeth'. But in his face was

CHAPTER 15

He was tall and long-legged, long-armed and long-fingered. He stood with a tense energy, seeming ready to explode into action at any second. His pale face was lined with brutal experience and seamed with old scars, but his gray eyes were keen and cool. His beard and hair were silver, trimmed short and neat. Dark leather armor, not unlike Sol's, encased his chest; the only exposed flesh was on his pale, sinew-knotted arms. Leather bracers protected his forearms from wrist to elbow and were dyed the same striking indigo as Jordan's vest. The winged man spoke to her in a foreign tongue and Jordan recognized the words as sounding similar to the dialect she'd heard from the people in Nishpat.

"Do you speak English?" she asked, her voice hoarse. She coughed to clear it. Her pulse was still thrumming like mad. Jordan released one hand from Sol's back to wipe her hair from her eyes and the sweat from her brow. Sol lay with a terrifying stillness beneath her pressing hand.

The man looked surprised. "Since when do girls from The Conca prefer to speak English?" His accent was strange but not unpleasant. His voice was deep and seemed to rumble from his chest like a rolling boulder. He rolled his 'r's, which made Jordan think of a Scottish brogue.

"I'm not from The Conca," Jordan answered. She covered her nose as the stench of the dead harpy drifted toward her on the breeze. Her eyes watered.

The man wiped the harpy blood from his blades on tufts of grass, then produced a rag from his pocket and cleaned off the rest. "No? You're wearing the color."

"Sol bought me some clothes in Nishpat." Jordan looked down at Sol and the bandages around his torso dark with blood. "This is Sol." Jordan swallowed hard at the ashen color of her companion's face.

"And you?" The stranger replied. "What name are you?"

"Jordan." Her body trembled and her muscles felt fatigued from being shot through with adrenalin. She held out a hand to the their rescuer. "Where I'm from, we shake hands when we make a new friend." She only realized afterward that her hand was bloody, but it was too late to withdraw it.

The man looked down like he needed a second to remember what to do with it. His expression cleared and he stepped forward and took it, seeming not to mind the blood. The skin of his palm was thick and calloused. They shook.

"Toth," he offered in return.

"Sorry about the blood," she said.

"Blood is a consequence of my job." He dismissed her apology, wiping his hand on the rag he still held. His eyes were a light gray, but bright enough to be startling. Black kohl had been applied on his bottom lid with a much more practiced hand than Jordan's. With his enormous leathery wings folded up behind him and the long black claws at the tops of his wings curving inward to make a sinister frame for his face, their defender cut a terrifying figure. With the multitude of throwing and fighting weapons strapped to his body, he gave new meaning to the phrase 'armed to the teeth'. But in his face was an intelligence and an unexpected kindness that put Jordan at ease.

"Where are you headed?" he asked.

"To Charra-Rae," said Jordan. She looked down at Sol and her stomach clenched with worry. "It's even more important that we get there as quickly as possible now. From what I understand, they have all kinds of healing magic."

She looked up at Toth. *This is no time to be shy, Jordan. Sol's life hangs in the balance.* "Would you accompany us there?" she asked. "He's one of you."

Toth blinked in surprise and then belted out a laugh, startling Jordan. The sound was deep and genuine and the smile transformed him into someone she could almost envision bouncing babies on a knee. "You don't need to lie to get me to escort you. You're wearing the indigo; that's enough. You could have put in for an escort before you left Nishpat."

"I'm not lying," Jordan said, affronted. "He's winged, too. He just lost his wings—" and there she halted. Sol had warned her not to speak about the portal. She changed her approach. "If you help me get him up on a horse, you'll see for yourself that his vest is just like yours, with the openings at the back."

Toth grunted. "Well if he's a Nycht, he's not from around here. I know all the Nychts in The Conca, even the ones way up at Praiff."

Nychts? Jordan absorbed this thoughtfully but hesitated to ask him to define the term. She assumed he meant his kind. It seemed that tipping strangers off that she wasn't from around here could be dangerous business. "It seems inadequate," said Jordan, "but thank you for saving our lives."

"Thank the treaty," Toth answered. He jerked his chin toward the unconscious Sol. "I'm not sure I came along soon enough to save his, though there'll be no penalty if he dies. He's not wearing any indigo."

Jordan blinked as the understanding finally dawned. She felt dumb. It had been staring her in the face. "That's why you saved us? Because of the indigo?"

Toth put his now shining weapons back in their holsters. "There is an agreement between the Nychts of The Conca and its human citizens. Those who wear the indigo are protected and defended."

"Not for free, I'll wager."

"Nothing is ever free. The Nychts of The Conca aren't farmers or tailors, but we need food and clothing as much as anyone." Toth jerked his head toward the harpy carcass. "Even those abominations know about the indigo by now. That's why she only went after your friend." He nodded toward Sol.

"Actually, she came after me and the horses first. He diverted her."

Toth grunted his surprise. "Bold. Perhaps she thought she could get away with it. I've been up against her before. She was a real battle-axe and crafty." Jordan thought he spoke of his foe with a kind of respect.

Toth's eyes flashed up to the grove where Jordan had tied up the two horses. Their heads were up, eyes trained on Toth and their ears twitched forward and back. They were much calmer now and seemed to understand that the danger had passed.

Toth took out a serrated blade and strode toward a grove of trees. "I'll make up a soirat for him," he said. "He's in no condition to be draped over the back of a horse like a sack of puskers." He stopped and put a hand to his chest and then to his belt like he was looking for something. He retrieved a small bottle from a pocket at his hip and turned back to hand it to Jordan. "Put this on his wounds; it'll close them up temporarily." He turned and went to the grove.

Jordan held the small, amber glass bottle up to the light. A slow-moving liquid shifted inside it. She knelt beside Sol and began to untie the bandages she'd put on him.

"Sol," she said near his ear. "Can you hear me? Can you wake up?"

His eyes cracked open ever so slightly. "Awake," he croaked. He made to lift his head.

"Stay down," Jordan said. "The less you move the better. We'll get you to Charra-Rae, he's going to help us." Jordan blew out a breath. "Thank God."

Sol's icy blue eyes focused beyond Jordan on the Nycht that was now sawing at a branch in the copse of trees. "Nycht," he grated out.

"Yes and that brings me to a question." Jordan had the bandage off and uncorked the small bottle. She upturned it over the nasty ragged wound and watched the gel-like substance crawl down the bottle. "Why didn't you get some indigo for yourself to wear? You knew it would protect you."

Sol gave a soft grunt and closed his eyes.

Jordan had her suspicions. "Ego can get you—" she paused, fascinated, as she watched the gel drop onto the wound and begin to move. The gel spread out to the edges of the torn skin and turned opaque. The substance began to shrink, pulling the edges together and forming a lumpy seam. "Killed." She looked at the bottle. "This stuff is amazing!"

"Nyop-" Sol took a breath.

"Nyopsis," she finished. The same stuff Sol had put on the horses' wounds. "I should start an import business to Earth." She tied the bandages closed again.

"Doesn't last." The words came out on a whisper and ended with a grunt of pain.

"Yeah, Toth said it was temporary." She stoppered the bottle. "That's our new friend over there."

Sol's eyes opened and locked on Toth's back. His mouth flattened into a grim line. Jordan thought maybe Sol was going to say something important.

"Water," Sol rasped.

Jordan retrieved the water pouch and held it for Sol while he drank. The sounds of Toth sawing and ripping branches apart echoed off the cliffs.

Toth approached the horses and Jordan followed, leaving Sol's side only because she wasn't sure how the animals would react to the newcomer. But they stayed calm and even put their muzzles in Toth's armpit by way of hello. They stamped their feet and whinnied, tossing their heads, their ears perked forward. It was almost like they were greeting an old friend.

Toth spoke in his language to one of the horses, his voice soothing. He looked at Jordan over his shoulder. "Can you live without this saddle?"

"I guess. Why?"

"I need it for parts." Toth undid the saddle and pulled it off the animal's back. "Bring him."

Jordan led the bay to where Toth had constructed a strange looking frame. She watched as Toth sliced apart the saddle, taking the leather straps and parts of the fenders and skirt. He lashed the scraps to the frame he'd created and mounted the whole lot on the back of the bay. It was almost a bed, with two flexible branches running down on either side of the horse's back and more woven branches making a sort of netting.

"Looks like you've done this before," Jordan commented, impressed.

Toth grunted in answer and went to Sol. "Can you stand, lad?"

Sol's eyes blazed and he clenched his jaw and moved to sit upright. Jordan suspected he didn't much care to be called 'lad'.

Jordan helped Sol take his weapons holsters off; they'd only cause him pain when he lay in the soirat. She got an arm under his shoulder. "Speaking of having done this before…" she said. It wasn't that long ago that she was helping a wounded Sol to hobble across her lawn.

With Jordan's help, Sol made his way to the horse and Toth boosted him up onto the back of the bay where he could lay with his wounded side up. Jordan used what was left of her tattered cloak to make a pillow for under his chest. Turmoil and pain bleached Sol's face of color. No doubt it was embarrassing for someone of Sol's ability and stature to be rescued and then reduced to cargo.

Jordan handed Sol a waterskin. "Do you need anything else?"

Sol shot her a glare.

Jordan held up her palms. "Sorry." She watched Toth walk away to get the gray horse. "Try to be a teensy bit grateful. Without him, we'd be dead."

It was the wrong thing to say, even if it was true.

Sol shot her a glare that would melt rock, lay his head back and closed his eyes, his mouth a tight line.

Jordan bit her cheeks against a smile. *Apparently, he really hates being vulnerable. Maybe he even blames me for this whole predicament. I didn't* mean *to open a portal. What's that saying about 'the road to hell...'?* She turned away, but a grunt from Sol made her turn back.

Sol gestured to the bushes just off the road. "My satchels."

Jordan retrieved them and dropped them over her head and shoulder, letting them rest across her body. Sol gazed at her and dropped his outstretched hand. Jordan waited for him to ask for them—a request she'd refuse, since they'd be safer with her. After a second's hesitation, he didn't protest. His expression softened and he lay his head down on the soirat.

Jordan gathered Sol's discarded, bloody knives from the dirt, as well as his sword. She cast about for the spear but it was nowhere to be seen. She cleaned the weapons the way Toth had done his and returned the throwing knives to their places in Sol's leather holster. Considering the weapons, she took a moment to strap them to herself. Better her than Sol, at this point.

Toth brought her the gray and she swung up onto her back.

"Do we just leave her there?" Jordan asked, glancing at the harpy carcass.

"Her own kind will take care of her," said Toth with a grunt. He took the bridle of the bay and led the odd group onward as they continued north.

* * *

JORDAN WATCHED the back of the amazing winged mercenary for an hour, replaying his awe-inspiring aerobatic feats in her mind. Finally, she nudged her horse up beside him. She peeked in at Sol on her way by. His eyes were closed, his color pale, but his chest rose and fell steadily,

"So," she said casually, keeping pace with Toth as he walked. "What's your story?"

He glanced up at her and then back down as he led the horse between a cluster of thorny bushes. "My story? You wish to converse?"

"Of course," Jordan replied. "You're..." Her eyes skimmed his enormous leathery wings, the long hooked claws at the tops of them, the muscular chest and arms and the seemingly countless straps and pockets for holding all kinds of weaponry. "A force."

Toth chuckled. "You should meet my brother."

"You have a brother?"

"Eleven brothers."

"Good heavens. Your poor mother. Any sisters?"

"Four sisters."

"And where are you in that enormous lineup?"

The corner of his mouth twitched. "Seventh."

"And are they all deadly, too?"

He shook his head. "Caje and I are the only mercenaries in our family. The rest of them are still in Rodania." Jordan thought that from the way he said it, Toth wasn't overly happy about this.

She shifted on her horse in an effort to ease her aching thigh muscles. "That's where Sol is from, too."

Toth nodded. "Most of us are."

Jordan chewed her lip. "When I said Sol was one of you, I meant winged."

Toth looked up at her.

"But he referred to himself as Arpak, not Nycht. I was wondering—"

Toth brought the horse to a halt, his lined face registering first surprise, then annoyance.

Jordan's gray halted and she lurched forward on the horse. "... what the difference was. What? What's wrong?"

Toth started walking again with a sour look. "Should have known," he muttered. "Should have let him die."

"Why? You don't like Arpaks?"

Toth huffed a dry laugh. "More like they don't like us. Nychts are second-class citizens in Rodania. It's the reason the rebels left. The Arpaks have always thought themselves superior."

Jordan's brow furrowed. The memory of Toth facing off with the harpy rose to mind. Capable. Frightening. "How does that make any sense?"

"They justify it in lots of ways," Toth said. "Nychts are nocturnal, so unless we force ourselves to go against our nature, we miss out on all of the goings on during the day—which is when all the business is done and big decisions are made." Toth got more animated, sweeping his hand in the air as he talked. "Arpaks will tell you that they're more intellectual, while Nychts are biologically better as laborers and soldiers. The structure of Strix society is designed to put Arpaks into positions of power - politicians, scholars, philosophers, doctors, lawyers, bureaucrats–it's all dominated by Arpaks." Toth shook his head.

"They won't admit it, but they'll block any Nycht who wants to make something more of themself than a soldier or a tradesperson." He shot Jordan a look and raised a scarred finger. "Don't be fooled. They'll act like they're all for equality, but they'll cut off any Nycht who might be good enough to climb their way up in society—and then blame it on our natural inferiority." Toth's voice rose and fell with passion. "But they can't fool us. If anyone doubts it, all they need to do is look at the Council."

Jordan had a feeling she knew where this was going. The problem was an ancient one. Prejudice. "Let me guess. They're all Arpaks?"

"Every last one." Toth said through clenched teeth.

"The Council? That's—"

"Strix government." Toth turned his head away from Jordan and spat. "Sorry," he wiped his mouth.

Jordan unhooked her waterskin from the pommel of her saddle and handed it to Toth.

"Thanks." He took a couple of long draughts, his throat working and then he handed the waterskin back to Jordan. "I know where all the best water is everywhere along The Conca, so I never carry any with me. But I'm also never earthbound."

Jordan's mind was hooked by the Nycht/Arpak conflict. *Is what Toth said about the inequality true, or exaggerated?* She remembered the grim look on Sol's face when he learned that they'd been rescued by a Nycht. *Every conflict has two sides.* She wondered what Sol would have to say about the Nychts and made a mental note to ask him when he was well. "Does a Strix have to campaign for a position on The Council?"

Toth nodded. "All except for the king."

"So you have a monarch, as well?"

"He's not my king!" Toth said, passionately.

"Arpak?" Jordan guessed.

Toth bowed his head toward her, his lip curling with a sneer. "Of course."

"Interesting." Jordan was fascinated. It wasn't any different than the prejudices that women or non-whites have faced throughout all of history on Earth. "So when a Nycht campaigns for Council—"

Toth barked a laugh. "Nychts aren't *allowed* to run for Council." The look he shot her was full of acid.

"They can't even try?"

Toth shook his head. "See what I mean? When challenged about it, Arpaks hide behind our 'biological differences' and 'natural strengths', but, believe me, they have no interest in ever giving Nychts a place at the table."

"I'm beginning to understand why you left," Jordan said. "But you never tried coming together to fight it?"

"No point," Toth grunted. "The Arpaks are too powerful and have no desire to change."

"Do they allow women on the council?"

Toth looked surprised. "Of course! Half of the seats are reserved for female Arpaks."

"Oh."

"In fact, the original Council, formed almost seventeen hundred years ago, was all women. Men were only given a place one thousand years later." Toth scratched his head. "If my history is correct. It wasn't my best subject."

This just gets more and more interesting, thought Jordan. "So the Arpaks *can* change the rules. They *could* be convinced—"

"There are those who are trying," Toth admitted. "I wish them luck; it would be easier to pass through Golpa than to change that law."

"Golpa?"

"A massive underground network of caves full of harpies. Some say that's where the first harpy was bred."

Jordan's skin crawled at the thought of a place that hosted more than one of those dreadful creatures. "Where is it?"

Toth jerked his chin straight ahead, toward The Conca that stretched out endlessly in front of them. "All the way at the North end."

"You said 'bred'. Someone is breeding them?"

Toth shrugged. "Maybe. They're a hybrid." He spat off to the side again. "'Scuse me. Revolting creatures. That's a crossbreed that should never have happened. It never would have happened without some kind of help."

"A hybrid of what?"

"Greater-vulture and dragon," Toth answered.

Jordan gasped. "You have dragons?!"

Toth narrowed his eyes up at her. "Just where are you from, Jordan?"

"Uh," she stumbled. "Not…here."

"Clearly." He raised his brows but didn't pry.

Jordan heard sounds of shifting from the horse-mounted bed and she pulled her horse back. "Sol," Jordan gasped, alarmed. His skin had turned a sickly gray and a sheen of sweat covered his face, neck and arms. His long dark hair was soaked and sticking to his scalp.

"We need to stop," said Jordan. "He doesn't look good."

Toth kept the horse moving. "That'll be the infection setting in," he said calmly. "There's a place to stop up ahead."

"Infection?" Jordan echoed.

"Harpy claws are filthy; some say poisonous, though I don't think anyone's proven it."

"You don't sound concerned." Jordan pulled up alongside Toth again.

Toth lifted a shoulder. "Some live. Some die."

"What?" Jordan halted her horse. Her gut began to churn as she watched Sol pass by her. She dismounted and left the gray to follow along behind the brown horse. She jogged up to Toth. "He can't die. What can we do? Don't you have some kind of potion or something?" She fought to quell the rising panic. "Something else like the nyopsis, but for infection?"

"I'm not a doctor," said Toth. "And Strix don't have magic."

"Ugh," she groaned. "Don't remind me." Frustration rose at Toth's indifference. "Have you ever been scratched by a harpy?"

"Many times. First time is always the worst. Best thing for him is to find a doctor, or an Elf." Toth waggled his head back and forth as though weighing options. "I don't know of any doctors between here and Charra-Rae, so we might as well continue on." He shot her a cocked eyebrow. "If you're sure the Elves of Charra-Rae are the ones you need to see."

"Well, I've no idea," Jordan cried. "Sol just said they were the closest." She didn't like how he'd asked that last question. "Why? What's wrong with the Elves of Charra-Rae?"

"Maybe nothing," Toth said, as he turned down a narrow path through a grassy slope leading to the bank of a stream. "But there's a lot of people who go into Charra-Rae that don't come out again."

Jordan's feet rooted to the spot and her jaw gaped as she watched Toth and the gelding that carried Sol meander toward the water. "Great," she muttered and stomped after them.

CHAPTER 16

*J*ordan stood on her tiptoes atop a rock next to the gelding as she cleaned Sol's wounds and used the nyopsis to close them up again. As the nyopsis aged, the seal began to open but it was the best they could do for Sol until they got to Charra-Rae. She had to peel the first batch of gel away like it was dried glue and she cringed as the bleeding started again.

Her eyes shot to his ashen face and her chin wobbled. She fought to get her emotions under control as she leaned forward and put a hand to his cheek. "Don't die on me, Sol," she whispered. She held a cool damp cloth to his forehead as the nyopsis closed his wounds like a strange gooey zipper. He was hot with fever.

"How long until Charra-Rae?" she asked Toth, who was waiting patiently nearby, scanning the dimming skies.

"Depends on the route we take. Passage of Skeel is easier, but takes longer and is more dangerous. Climbing out after Usenno is harder but faster." He turned slowly, scanning the skies and cliffs they'd left behind them. "Your choice."

"We need to take the fastest way possible," she replied,

covering the torn terrain of Sol's back with fresh strips taken from her cloak. She tied them tightly. "I don't know if he'll survive this infection." Her voice trembled with exhaustion and emotion.

"He will survive if he is strong," Toth said, helping Jordan down from the rock. "Drink. And fill your waterskin. You'll need it."

Usenno, as it turned out, was a tiny cluster of a dozen farmhouses surrounded by fields of yellow flowers. If Jordan had been less worried, she would have grilled Toth for details about the crops and lifestyles of the people who lived there. As it was, they focused on feeding and watering the horses and Jordan tried to get Sol to wake up enough to eat and drink something. She failed. Sol would not be woken, but lay in his strange sickbed, breathing weakly and cooking with fever. Jordan's body ached and her eyes drooped with exhaustion—but as night fell, she pressed them onward and Toth was happy to oblige. The Nycht seemed inexhaustible and Jordan wished for some of his resilience.

Sometime in the middle of the night, they finally stopped to snatch a few hours' rest. It wasn't enough, but it had to be and they were up and moving again before the sun was up.

Around midmorning, Toth stopped the horses, his neck craning upward.

"What?" Jordan croaked from beside the gray mare. She felt bad riding the horse, though the mare seemed to be handling the walking much better than Jordan was. The mare turned her head and nuzzled Jordan's side as if telling her to sit down.

"Here we climb," Toth said.

"Climb?" Jordan echoed weakly. Her eyes followed the narrow switchbacks up the mountainside. The road was dusty, steep and filled with rocks the size of bowling balls. "What's wrong with that way?" She pointed down to the much flatter, much friendlier-looking valley bottom.

"That's the Passage of Skeel," grunted Toth, bending to check the gelding's hooves and ankles. Both horses had scabbed over nicely and their wounds were well on the way to fully healed. "You can't see them, but that earth is full of cankerworms."

"Do I even want to know what those are?"

"No," Toth stood. "You don't. They siphon away the years of your life while you sleep."

Jordan shuddered. "Up we go then." She trudged towards the trailhead. "Wait, can the horses do this?"

"We'll find out."

The going was slow, but the horses managed the switchbacks better than Jordan could have hoped for. She refused to ride the mare on this treacherous terrain, so she trudged along at the rear, tripping on rocks and trying not to lose her mind with fear as the valley floor got further and further away. Even at the slow, laborious pace the group set, it was remarkable the height they were able to gain in an hour. The gelding took every step as though he knew what was at stake and not for the first time on this journey, Jordan's heart burst with respect for the nobility of the horses Sol had rescued.

She'd begun to hum tunelessly to herself to pass the time and distract from the seemingly endless hairpin turns and stretches of trail traversing along the mountainside. She was so glazed and winded that when the horses stopped, she walked straight into the hindquarters of the mare. The mare looked back at Jordan and snorted at her as if to say, *'We're at the top. Pay attention.'*

"Here we are," said Toth, "This is the border of Charra-Rae."

"Really?" Jordan passed the horses and stood by the Nycht at the grassy top of the cliff overlooking The Conca to goggle out at the scene before them.

Sweeping away on a seemingly endless, rolling terrain was a lush forest of all the colors one would ascribe to tropical water: from bright teals to dark greens and everything in between. Late afternoon light danced with moving shadows as wind swirled through the broken cloud cover overhead. It seemed the canopy here changed color far more drastically than with forests on Earth; it was not unlike watching the ocean as it shifted under the power of the wind and currents. Jordan squinted. It really did look like the leaves were moving in currents—not back and forth, like they were rooted, but continuously, like flowing water. But as her vision locked onto these strange moving patches of color, it was simply a trick of her eyes and the leaves weren't really flowing like water. The effect was dizzying.

"It's beautiful," breathed Jordan, swaying a little on her feet. She wasn't sure if the vertigo was from the never-ending vista before her, or the fact that they'd just climbed never-ending and near-impossible switchbacks.

"Yes. It's beautiful." Toth's brow furrowed. "And possibly deadly."

Jordan contemplated the concern on Toth's face. "What's in there? Besides Elves?"

"I don't know. I've never gone into Charra-Rae. It's outside The Conca, so there's never been a reason to. The stories tend to keep people away."

Jordan wasn't too tired to catch the subtext in Toth's statement. "Does that mean the indigo is no longer in effect here?" The thought of venturing into Charra-Rae by herself with an unconscious Sol, while trying to find the Elves was enough to make her knees go weak.

Toth looked at her with a wrinkled brow. "Technically." He led the gelding to a narrow stream that burbled from the ground and ran downhill through a rocky bed. "I'll go with you until I can pass you off to the Elves."

Jordan closed her eyes with relief. "That's very kind. Thank you."

"Welcome," Toth grunted, his back to her as he stroked the gelding's neck. The mare wandered up on his other side to get a drink. Toth spoke so softly, Jordan wasn't sure if he was speaking to her or the horses. "It would be heartless to leave you here alone. Nychts aren't heartless."

Jordan found this comment interesting and would have mined for meaning if she weren't so exhausted. "So, now what?" Jordan managed. She wanted nothing more than to collapse in the grass and sleep for days. But as long as Sol was still breathing —and he was—they had to keep moving.

"Now we walk." Toth made a clicking sound and grasped the gelding's bridle. They began to move downhill toward the trees, the mare following of her own accord.

"For how long?" Jordan asked, falling into step beside the mare as she high-stepped through the long grasses. "How do we find the Elves?"

Toth shot her an enigmatic smile. "One doesn't find Elves. We walk until they find us."

They made their way down the slope to the tree line. The tree trunks curved and gnarled in every direction. The limbs of these trees were like arms winding their way up to the canopy far above and taking the longest possible route to get there. The bark was so dark and damp that it was nearly black. As they passed from the grass into Charra-Rae, Jordan thought she heard a sound similar to a power grid being shut down—a sort of long, deep, descending sigh. Then her ears popped. She looked over at Toth, who met her eyes. The horses tossed their heads and the gray whinnied, which echoed through the trees.

"What was that?" Jordan kept her voice low, though she wasn't sure why.

"Magic," said Toth. Jordan could see the blonde hairs on Toth's forearms standing at attention and goosebumps swept her own flesh. "They know we're here now." He took a deep breath and continued walking, his leathery wings shook outward and then closed up tight again. "Lets just hope they'll let us leave when the time comes."

Jordan swallowed and stepped in behind Toth and the bay, as

the trees prevented them from walking side by side. The air became richly humid and heavy with the scent of soil and mulch. There was another smell on the air and Jordan inhaled to try and identify it. "What is that fragrance? Reminds me of sandalwood." She sniffed again. "Or something else spicy."

"Gersher fungus," said Toth, pointing upward. "They're difficult to spot from the bottom, but their tops are bright pink. It's a product of Charra-Rae. I think they trade and sell them."

Jordan craned her neck. They were difficult to see, but she soon found what Toth was pointing to. Little round mushroom-like growths sprouted from tree limbs up high in the canopy. A couple of the fungi grew on an angle and Jordan could just make out slivers of fuchsia on their tops. "They don't grow below thirty feet, or what?"

Toth shrugged. "Something like that. If there are any in reach, don't touch them. I don't think the Elves would appreciate it."

But they didn't see any growing lower than about three stories up. Jordan soon got used to the scent and no longer noticed it. As they walked, she and Toth fell into silence. Jordan found herself in a constant state of dopey distraction as she took in the foreign forestscape around them. It seemed to her that the tree branches were moving in her periphery; not in the way a branch normally would, waving in the wind, but rather like its own separate entity. When she'd look directly, though, there was nothing amiss. She began to play games with herself, trying to memorize a pattern of branches, looking away, then looking back to see if they'd moved. But by the time her eyes found the same trees, she couldn't access the memory of the way they'd looked. It was endlessly fascinating and more than a little disconcerting. *My exhaustion must be to blame,* Jordan thought uneasily.

They stopped for a rest several hours later. Sol hadn't been conscious since they'd left Usenno and Jordan found herself forcing positive thoughts through her mind. *He's going to be fine. The Elves will appear at any moment and they'll save him.* She tried putting the waterskin to Sol's lips, but there was no response. His breathing was becoming shallow and the sounds of mucous in his chest were getting worse. The skin on his arms was clammy to the touch, yet burning up on his head and neck. Toth waited patiently while she changed Sol's bandages and applied the last of the nyopsis to keep the wounds sealed up.

"I hope they show themselves soon," Jordan muttered. "If he dies..." She didn't finish the sentence out loud but continued to think: *Who will deliver the message that might be so important? Even if I might be able to do it, how would I? Where is it going and into whose hands does it need to be delivered? Will Sol ever wake up to pass on the information, or will he quietly slip away without warning? He could die at any moment.* She felt sick when she thought about it. Not only for the logistics of his death; she could admit it to herself—she had come to care for her oft-grouchy companion.

She and Toth let the horses graze on the thick moss along the narrow winding trail for a time. Toth pulled a sack from one of his endless pockets and sat on a stone. He opened the little bag and held it out to Jordan.

"What is it?" Jordan sat down beside him.

"Pinzo."

Jordan gave him a grim smile. "Not sure why I even bother asking." She dipped her fingers into the sack, pulling out a handful of small wrinkly purple balls. She sniffed them. They smelled like berries, so she popped them into her mouth. They were chewy and bittersweet. They ate and rested as long as they dared, then got up and moved on.

The sound of a waterfall in the distance perked the horses' ears forward. The air grew cool and humid as they drew close to the cascade. When the waterfall came into sight, it almost made Jordan's heart stop. It filled her ears with thunder, while a powerful vibration thrummed under the soles of her boots. Toth came to stand beside her and gaze at the immense water feature.

Their hair and skin quickly became damp from the mist in the air.

They stood on the banks of a sparkling river as it poured over stones that looked like they'd been put there on purpose. The boulders made a bridge across the rushing water. A few hundred meters away, a huge churning pool of turbulent foam roared and gurgled. The cascade itself was as tall as a skyscraper and wider than a city block. The river in front of them was just one of several spilling downhill from the base of the waterfall. The parallel lines of the rivers had boulevards of grasses and trees growing up in between them. Only someone very powerful, or with powerful magic, could have set the boulders in their places. They looked to weigh several tons each. But it wasn't the rows of rivers or the pathway of rocks that made Jordan's eyes widen and her head tilt back until her neck creaked.

The waterfall poured over the face of a huge stone city. Balconies, arched windows, columns, turrets and towers all ran with streams of white water. Bright teal moss grew on damp stone faces. Carved gargoyles, crows and other sculpted beasts spilled streams of water. A huge dragon's head, poking out from a curtain of water, hinted at how big the body hiding behind the veil might be. Black caverns appeared here and there, suggesting caves and hidden places behind the falls.

"What I'd give for a camera," Jordan breathed.

"A what?" Toth also couldn't tear his eyes from the sight before them.

"How did this happen? It must have been a natural disaster or something. This city is magnificent."

"I never knew there was such a place," said Toth. "I suppose if an Elf ever shows up, we could ask them." He ran a hand through his wet hair, making it stand up in short silvery spikes. "Shall we cross?"

"Can the horses do it?" Jordan scanned the tops of the boulders, trying to work out the risk. The gelding had the addition of a sick man tottering on his back.

Toth's hand on her arm made her follow his gaze up to the waterfall. She took a breath.

Standing in one of the dark spaces, with water parting over her head and falling away without getting her wet, was an Elf.

CHAPTER 17

She stood there without moving for so long that Jordan wondered if the Elf was a statue she'd simply missed spotting. Her skin was the same color as the stones, a sort of soft alabaster gray. She was wearing a teal dress in the same shade as the moss growing on the stones around her. But the shadows in the folds of her knee length skirt changed as the clothing shifted, giving her away. From a distance, the features of her face weren't clear, but when she stepped forward and out of the shadow of the falls, Jordan could see high, arched brows, a fine-boned face and long white hair. The elf stopped on the ledge, looking down at them, expressionless. Jordan's heart thudded in her ears. Relief and anxiety mingled in her blood making her hands tremble.

Suddenly, the Elf turned her back and the curtains of water closed together behind her.

"No," Jordan whispered. Then louder, "Don't go!" She stepped forward and put a hand up, but it was too late. The Elf was gone.

"Just wait," said Toth quietly.

They stood still on the banks of the river. Jordan's knees quaked as her eyes scanned the cascade, searching for another glimpse of the Elf.

They didn't have to wait long. Another curtain of water opened at ground level and she reappeared. She stepped out and to the side of the dark opening. She made a welcoming gesture with one arm, inviting them inside. To get to her, though, they'd have to cross a treacherous scattering of boulders covered in moss. There was no nicely-placed pathway leading up to where she was.

Jordan and Toth shared a look. Jordan opened her mouth to ask if they were supposed to carry Sol and leave the horses on the banks when the brown horse carrying Sol walked toward the Elf.

"Wait!" Jordan put her hand out but it was too late. The gelding passed her and stepped out over the water. His hooves made a sound like he was stepping onto hollow wood and he walked straight out over the water on some invisible surface. Jordan's hand flew to her mouth and her eyes went wide. The mare followed the gelding and soon both of them seemed to be hanging in midair, making their way up a slight incline to their waiting hostess. Jordan thought she heard the Elf murmur something to the horses as she allowed them to pass. Sol and the gelding disappeared behind the falls and the mare followed. When the mare's tail had disappeared, the Elf turned her head toward them as if to say, '*aren't you coming?*'

Toth turned to Jordan. "She's waiting for you." He didn't seem nearly as shocked at this magic.

"You're not coming?" Jordan had been bracing herself for it, but it still hit her like a punch in the gut.

"I have already been gone from The Conca for too long. You've reached your destination; this is where I leave you." He spoke simply, unemotionally.

"But—" But, there was nothing else to say. He was right. She didn't need him anymore. He had a life to get back to. A job. Jordan closed her mouth and bit her lips between her teeth as a rush of emotion took her by surprise. She threw her arms around Toth and squeezed him. She wanted to say thank you, but if she did, she'd burst into tears and that would be embarrassing for both of them.

Toth stiffened, surprised by her display of affection. Humans in The Conca never showed this kind of appreciation for an escort. The service was expected. There was hardly even a 'thank you' for the job done. Slowly, he put his arms around Jordan's narrow figure and squeezed her back. His eyes drifted up to the waiting Elf and he found himself wishing he could stay, just to make sure Jordan found her way out of here once Sol was healed. *If the Elves will even heal him.* A wave of protectiveness went through him and he let her go, taking a step back. It wasn't good to get attached to humans; it was better he leave her.

"How do I find you again?" Jordan said, her voice cracking.

Not only is she grateful, she seems to want a friendship. Toth's brow wrinkled. *That wouldn't be wise.* "Why would you need to find me?"

Jordan's eyes misted. "You saved us. We...we're friends." She hesitated. "Aren't we?"

Toth's eyes shuttered, like someone had pulled the blinds over a window. "Nychts and humans shouldn't be friends. We're trade partners. It's best kept that way." He jerked his chin at the Elf. "I don't imagine she's going to wait all day. Good luck, Jordan." He gave her the smallest smile and stepped back. He spread his wings and the sound of them opening was like the sails of a tall ship catching the wind.

"But..." she was at a loss for words. *That's it? After what we've been through together, what he's done for us? It doesn't seem right.*

With a few effortful strokes, Toth left the ground. He gave Jordan a final nod and climbed up toward the sky. Up above the canopy and past the edge of the waterfall, Jordan saw him catch an updraft and pick up speed. He disappeared over the tops of the trees. Jordan felt like she'd swallowed a bag of cold rocks. With a sigh of frustration, she stepped off the riverbank and felt the invisible solid footing beneath her. Without any further hesitation, she marched up to the Elf and walked through the open curtain of water.

* * *

THE TUNNEL JORDAN found herself in was damp and cool and her skin prickled with gooseflesh at the humid air that hugged her. The cave was long enough that the horses were only now reaching the end of it. Their hoofbeats sounded sharp on the stone and echoed back through the cavernous channel. The opening was a small circle of bright light at the other end. The sound of trickling water could be heard through cracks in the arched stone passageway. The Elf made so little sound that Jordan thought she must have stayed behind, but looking over her shoulder, Jordan started in surprise. The Elf was right behind her. Looking down, Jordan saw the reason for her soundlessness—she wore no shoes. Her feet were ghostly pale in the dim light.

"Hello," said Jordan. Her voice bounced off the walls.

The Elf faced her briefly. It was difficult to make out her expression in such darkness. There was no reply.

Jordan nearly stumbled at the steep drop off at the tunnel's exit. A narrow dirt ramp led from the tunnel's exit to the forest floor. The ramp had a gnarled wooden railing so covered in curling ivy that it seemed to be trying to choke the wood. The horses had slowed their pace to navigate the steep downhill, but were nearly at the bottom when Jordan stepped out of the tunnel. Two Elves took the horses' bridles and two more began to unstrap the rig that Toth had built.

"Please be careful, he's very sick," said Jordan, rushing to help. Sol's body barely jostled as the Elves lowered him and the whole soirat to the ground.

One of the Elves shot her a withering look that said *'Obviously'*.

"Many of the people who visit us are." The other spoke kindly and Jordan found that the sound of his voice plucked a string inside her, one that went on to vibrate even after he finished speaking.

"Can you help him?" Jordan knelt beside Sol and put her hand on his forehead. He was burning up. His breathing still sounded very shallow.

"That depends."

"On what?" Anxiety fluttered in her chest. She hadn't the first idea how to negotiate with Elves. What was it that Sol had in mind to pay them with? Gold?

"Not what," said the Elf, standing up. "Who." His eyes lifted and Jordan followed his gaze.

A tall, slender Elf with long red hair stood at the edge of the clearing just a few feet away. Jordan hadn't noticed her approach. She had skin the color of milk and her hair was a rich dark color, almost burgundy. Her widely spaced eyes were just a little too big to look human and they shone like sapphires.

"Welcome to Charra-Rae," she said. Her voice twanged an entirely different string inside Jordan than the male Elf's had. This one made her body buzz, which then dimmed rapidly to nothing. Jordan could feel her molars vibrate against one another in her head. It was a startling feeling but not entirely unpleasant. "You're not from The Conca."

"No. We're not." Jordan wondered how she knew that. Even Toth had been fooled by the indigo.

"You're a long way from Rodania," the Elf went on.

Jordan's brows shot up. *That's where Sol is from! But how could she possibly know that?* Sol had no wings to reveal his species. Together, Sol and Jordan looked no different from any other human couple. Jordan began to wonder if these Elves had some kind of mind-reading ability. Toth's warning that people entered Charra-Rae but didn't leave rang in her memory. She shoved the warning away. She was here now and while these Elves were a bit disconcerting, she didn't feel like they were dangerous. The Elf went on before Jordan could answer.

"I'm Sohne." She dropped her chin slightly but kept her strange eyes on Jordan.

"I'm Jordan and this is Sol." Jordan shifted from foot to foot. "Please, we need your help. I'm afraid Sol is dying."

"He won't die," said Sohne. She lifted a hand and signalled to the two Elves who had stepped back and stood watching.

Relief flooded Jordan. "Oh, thank you." She closed her eyes in gratitude.

The elven men came forward and picked Sol up. They began to carry him through the trees toward some lights Jordan could see flickering in the distance. Sohne followed them and Jordan fell in step beside her. She wanted to ask how things worked when people showed up needing help. Based on what Sol had said, the Elves didn't just help out of the goodness of their hearts. But before she could organize her thoughts to form a question, the elven city appeared, rendering her speechless for the second time that day.

The thick forest ended and a new terrain began. The ground had broken off or been removed, leaving a grassy ledge. Below them was a rolling landscape of tall trees and stone steps and walkways. A large body of water sparkled in the distance and she could make out elegant huts and buildings nestled among the foliage. Even the Elf-made structures were so organic-looking they seemed to have sprouted from the earth. There wasn't a straight line to be seen anywhere. Dwellings unlike any she had seen before snugged up against trees and streams; some shaped like lumpy, off-kilter huts and others like tall, elegant cones with arched windows. Torches flickered throughout the scene and lights illuminated windows. But the light was not warm and orange like firelight—more a bright blue-white, like starlight. Elves and a few other beings Jordan had never seen before, moved about, talking, working, sitting, or conversing. Some of them held scrolls open in front of them and seemed to be discussing a patch of undeveloped land off to the side.

Movement drew Jordan's eyes upward. High in the trees on a network of vine bridges, people and non-human creatures worked, cutting away the fungus Toth had told her about and gathering it into baskets on their backs.

The sound of footsteps behind her made Jordan turn. Sol, Sohne, and the two other elves had already descended the stone steps leading into the valley. Jordan had been standing there and gaping at the scene alone.

A slow-moving line of people walked by Jordan and down the steps. They were holding baskets filled with the gersher fungus and Jordan could finally see how bright the fuchsia tops of the mushrooms really were. They were so pigmented as to look fake; like they were colored with magic marker.

"Excuse me," she said to them as they passed.

None of them looked up, or acknowledged her in any way. Jordan's eyes narrowed. There was something eerie about these people. She realized that none of them were Elves. Many of them appeared to be human, but there were a few other species in amongst the crowd that Jordan couldn't identify. Shorter, stockier beings with pointed ears. *Perhaps trolls?* Every one of them had a look of sublime contentment on their face. They walked by single file, with a slow, matching gait. Jordan's forearms prickled as she watched them pass down the stairs and disappear one by one into the thicker trees on the left side of the valley.

When the last of them passed, she followed them down the stairs and went to the right, where she saw the two Elves who were carrying Sol disappear into a small, not-quite-round hut made of woven vines. The hut was dark, but as Jordan approached, that blue-white light appeared from inside and shone out from between the cracks. She followed them and when she arrived at the hut's entrance. The hut was a simple space with a stone table covered with leaves in the center. Slender torches with clear balls at the top of them lit the space and made Sol look even paler.

The Elves put Sol gently on the table. Sohne lay a hand over Sol's chest and then over his forehead. "He will need tonight to rest, once I've reversed the infection and the injury." Her voice twanged those strings inside Jordan and she felt the vibration all the way down her spine and through her legs. It even seemed like her feet buzzed against the ground. She scrunched up her toes inside her boots in an effort to stop the tickling.

"Oh. Kay," said Jordan. "Is there some sort of payment or negotiation we need to do first?"

"I'll deal with him when he's conscious. You and I can talk separately about yours," answered Sohne, coming around the table and putting a hand on her shoulder. Jordan was about to ask Sohne how she knew she even had a request, but she pulled Jordan toward the door. "Eohne will show you where you can spend the night. You must be exhausted."

Another female Elf with long, wavy, brunette hair appeared in the doorway. She seemed a little out of breath. "Sohne, you called?" Her skin was flushed and dewy and her hair looked damp. She wore simple homespun clothes; not a beautiful dress, like Sohne. Just simple pants that looked like they were made of linen and a sleeveless tunic the color of leaves, belted at the waist. Her long bare arms were sinewy and muscular and her fingernails were blunt. Small, odd tools hung from her belt on strings.

"This is Jordan," said Sohne. "Take care of her for the night." Sohne looked at Jordan. "You and I will talk tomorrow."

Jordan allowed Eohne to draw her away from the hut, but she looked back over her shoulder at Sol's form lying on the table. The hut's door closed and Sol and Sohne were hidden from view. Sol had made it sound like the Elves just did magic, but she got the impression that it wasn't as easy as just waving their fingers.

"Jordan." Eohne drew Jordan's attention away from the hut and the mysterious goings on inside it. "Where are you from?"

"We..." Sol's warning not to talk about portals rang in her head. "Came in from Nishpat."

Eohne shot her a look over her shoulder as they descended some uneven rock stairs and joined a path that took them deeper into the elven city. "But you're not from Nishpat. If my ears are tuned right, you're from Earth."

Jordan nearly tripped in the pathway and Eohne grabbed her elbow to steady her. "Wh-what?"

"Don't worry," laughed Eohne. "We don't have any interest in reporting illegal portal travel."

"How can you tell?"

"Your accent, of course," said Eohne as they walked along a narrow burbling stream. Evening sunlight filtered down through the canopy and lit the glen around them in a soft yellow glow. "I don't know where on Earth you're from," she continued. "I don't know it well, but I know all the accents of The Conca and beyond and yours isn't like any of them. It was a guess, but I can see from your face that I was right." It was too late to deny it.

Jordan's tired eyes were drawn up toward movement in the canopy overhead. People and other species clearly not human, traversed narrow walkways that were built around tree trunks and between the trees and that hung from ropes fastened to limbs high above. Jordan's eyes scanned their faces and she narrowed her eyes as she noticed the same vacant expressions worn by the line of workers who'd passed her earlier.

"Who are they?" Jordan asked.

"Harvesters," Eohne said. "Watch your step here."

Eohne turned off the path and began to climb through thick ferns. Foot-sized stones the color of blood gleamed through the lush greenery and Jordan followed, taking each stone step by step. Jordan was puffing by the time they reached an embankment leading to a path on another level. Arching over their heads was the root system of many trees, entangled and half covering a path that wound along a ledge.

"Why do they look so vacant?" asked Jordan as she followed behind Eohne on the narrow ledge. Roots dangled down and brushed the tops of their heads and draped over their shoulders. "Like they're brain-dead or something."

"They're inmates," Eohne said mildly.

"Inmates?" Jordan brushed aside the roots as they swung from Eohne's shoulders and into her own face. "Like, prisoners?"

The path grew even narrower; Eohne stopped walking and faced the wall of dirt. She braced her foot against a root and stepped up; as she did, her head disappeared into a hole. Jordan watched, narrowing her eyes as bits of dirt and dust fell from the overhang while Eohne climbed up through the root system and disappeared the rest of the way through the hole. Her voice came back a moment later. "Are you coming?"

Jordan frowned as she saw little black beetles scuttle through the dirt around the hole and watched a bright green earthworm poke its head, or maybe its butt, out of the dirt to feel around. "Not really a fan of creepy-crawlies," she muttered.

"What?"

"Nothing. Coming." She grasped the root system and began to climb. As her head cleared the hole, she saw an exquisitely built wooden house braced between five thick-trunked trees. Like everything else in Charra-Rae, the house had no straight lines and half of it was covered in thick ivy. Stone steps led to the arched front door and purple flowers with blossoms the size of Jordan's head lined the pathway. "Where are we?"

"This is my dwelling. You'll stay with me while you're here." She walked the steps to the door and Jordan followed, brushing dirt from her shoulders. "Welcome," said Eohne and let the two of them in.

The moment they passed the threshold, the blue-white lights illuminated the house, coming from sconces on the walls and long vines hanging down from the ceiling. Eohne's place was small and cozy, with a very tall ceiling and two lofts. At first glance, Jordan couldn't see how anyone could get up to the lofts; then she spotted a ladder of braided vines fastened to the wall.

Shelves covered in all kinds of curious objects Jordan couldn't name covered the back wall. There were jars filled with specimens of insects, old tatty books with cracked spines and falling out pages and a long column of floor-to-ceiling glass with bright yellow butterflies fluttering inside it. "Are you a scientist of some kind?" asked Jordan.

Eohne smiled. "More of an inventor, but I guess you could say I know something about science." She cocked her head. "Our kind of science, anyway. I don't think Earthling science and mine bear much of a resemblance."

"What are you working on?" Jordan approached the shelves and snooped among the items.

"Replicating the fungus that grows here by using magic," said Eohne, clasping her hands behind her back and watching Jordan inspect her workspace.

"And how is it going?" Jordan tapped a finger against a glass jar filled with large clear balls, which also looked to be made of glass.

Eohne frowned. "Not very well. Be careful with those, please."

"Eeep!" Jordan took a step back when a few of the glass balls sprouted legs and began to crawl up the inside of the jar. "What are they?"

"Messenger bugs," Eohne said. "I've been working on them for a few months now, but haven't come up with a better name for them than that."

"Are they alive?"

"Not in an organic sense, no, but they do have a kind of intelligence."

"How do they work?" Jordan stepped closer to the glass again and peered in at the bugs.

"Partially by frequency and partially by magic."

"Would they take a message to Earth?"

Eohne frowned and thought about this. "Yes, in theory. Though I've never tried it. And also to the in between–wherever they find the person's frequency.

Jordan was staring at Eohne, wearing an expression caught between shock and joy. Her exhaustion from the trip was momentarily forgotten.

"What?" Eohne asked at the bright look on Jordan's face.

"I didn't expect you to say 'yes'. Could I send a message to my father?"

A slow smile spread across Eohne's face. She'd never had reason to try sending the bugs anywhere outside of Oriceran. This was just the kind of experiment she loved. "Let's give it a try. We haven't got anything to lose."

CHAPTER 18

"Carry this," Eohne said, handing the jar of bugs to Jordan. She grabbed a second jar with another dozen bugs in it and an over-the-shoulder bag and handed them to Jordan as well. "We have to hike for a bit to get away from all the interference around here."

"We can't send the message from here?" Jordan asked, craning her neck to watch Eohne climb the vine ladder and disappear onto the first loft platform.

Eohne poked her head over the side and cocked an eyebrow. "Why, you have somewhere else you need to be tonight?"

"No." Jordan smiled up at Eohne. "I'm just from a generation of instant gratification."

"Ha!" Eohne disappeared again and Jordan heard some cupboard doors opening and closing and items being rooted through. "We have that same problem here. Why else do you think everyone comes to the Elves when they have a problem? Magic does things faster."

Jordan thought of Sol's wings and how they would take years to grow back if the Elves didn't help him. "Is there anything you can't do with magic?"

"Oh, tons of stuff!" Eohne said as she put a foot on the vine ladder. "Magic can do a lot, but it's not foolproof; it's not always predictable, either." Jordan watched Eohne climb down, her movements fluid as water. She landed on the floor in front of Jordan. "Sohne could get a message to your dad faster than I could."

"Really? Well, why don't we do that, then? It might be better than using your experimental prototypes…"

"It'll cost you a lot more to go through her, trust me." Eohne pulled her own shoulder sack over her head and headed for the door. Jordan followed.

"What will it cost me?"

"I don't know, you'd have to figure that out with her, but believe me, it wouldn't come cheap. Just like your friend's healing won't come cheap." Eohne climbed back down through the hole in the rooty overhang.

"And you?" Jordan called down through the hole. "What'll it cost me to use your messenger bugs?"

Eohne peered up at the girl she was rapidly beginning to like. "Nothing." She grinned. "You get to send a message to your father and I get to test my prototypes. It's…" she frowned, thinking. "What do they call it in English…?"

"A win-win?" Jordan supplied.

"Exactly." Eohne disappeared.

"Well, alright then," Jordan said and climbed down through the hole. "Let's do this."

Jordan followed Eohne back the way they'd come. Seeing the people harvesting fungus in the treetops made her recall what Eohne had said about them. "You said they're inmates," Jordan said, tripping over a root as she gaped upward into the canopy.

"Yes." Eohne picked up the pace as they hit the trail and headed back toward the waterfall.

"What did they do?" Jordan jogged to catch up to the long-legged Elf.

"Who knows?" said Eohne. "All kinds of things."

At the top of the stairs near the clearing where Jordan had first encountered Sohne, Jordan stopped and looked back over the scene, her eyes continually drawn upward by the movement in the canopy. "Why do they look so expressionless?"

"Hurry up," Eohne called from the cave entrance leading to the waterfall. "We don't want to be on the other side when darkness falls and its already late."

Jordan jogged to catch up to the Elf. "Why, what happens after dark?"

"Same thing that happens on Earth, I imagine." Eohne's voice echoed through the cave as the two women passed through the damp rocky tunnel. "Predators come out."

"Harpies?" Her mouth went dry and her stomach heaved at the thought of it.

"No, they don't come in here. They can't maneuver in tight trees. But there's plenty of other beasts to worry about."

"Such as?" Jordan began, but then stopped. "Nevermind, maybe it's better that I don't know. How far do we have to go?"

"Not far. There's an open glen less than an hour's walk from here that works for inter-Oriceran messages; should work for yours, too."

The sound of the waterfall grew loud as the women passed through the cavern. The water opened for them and closed behind them as they descended the invisible ramp to the river's edge. Eohne went first, passing over the river, looking like she was hanging in midair. It was then that Jordan noticed Eohne had a curved blade in a sheath strapped to her back. Jordan's hand went involuntarily to Sol's knives, which she still carried at her hips. They were supposed to make her feel secure, but she couldn't help but feel unsettled by them. Just having them meant there was a possibility she'd have to use them. Not a happy thought.

"I'll never get used to this," Jordan muttered as she looked down through her feet at the rapids below her. Vertigo swept over her at the bizarre visual and she stopped for a moment to close her eyes. She breathed a sigh of relief when her feet struck land again. Eohne was already ahead in the woods and Jordan jogged to catch up.

"You were saying?" Jordan prompted as she matched Eohne stride for stride. The Elf set a brisk pace and Jordan's heart pounded steadily.

"I wasn't saying anything." Eohne tossed over her shoulder.

"About the inmates. Why are they so expressionless?"

"Oh, them. People bring us their criminals, we befuddle them and put them to work." She shrugged. "It's pretty straightforward."

"Befuddle?"

"A kind of magical stupor. We call it gnashwit."

"So, that's what Toth was talking about," Jordan mused.

"Who?"

"The Nycht who brought me here. He said people go into Charra-Rae and don't come out."

"Oh. Yes."

"So, people bring you their criminals and, what? You try them and sentence them to years of labor?" Jordan moved in behind Eohne as the trail narrowed and became lined with thick ferns. They brushed back against Eohne's long legs and thwacked Jordan in the thighs. The fronds were so thick it almost hurt.

Eohne laughed. "No, it doesn't work like that."

"How does it work?" Jordan slowed a bit so the ferns would swing back without smacking against her.

"Gnashwit is permanent. And there is no trial; at least, not here. If someone has been brought here, we assume a trial has already been done."

Jordan stopped for a second in surprise. "How do you know for sure they are even criminals?"

"I don't know. It's up to Sohne. I'm not really involved with the gnashwits." Something in Eohne's voice gave Jordan pause. She sounded uncomfortable, defensive.

"You don't agree with it?" Jordan guessed. The thick ferns ended, the terrain became soft and the trees became more widely spaced. Jordan fell into step beside Eohne, looking over at the Elf. She hadn't answered yet. "Eohne," she prompted.

"Hmmm."

"You don't agree with it?"

Eohne glanced at Jordan, her dark eyes troubled. "I didn't want her to use the magic yet. Not until I could reverse it."

Jordan's brows shot up. "You *invented* gnashwit?"

Eohne nodded. "I didn't know it would get used this way." She sighed. "I guess it's better than the inmates getting executed. Isn't it?"

"I don't know," said Jordan. "What's it like?"

"I have no idea. It doesn't seem so bad from the outside." But the look on Eohne's face said she wasn't so sure. "They basically live the same day over and over again. At first when they come in, there are questions and some of them seem really traumatized. Eventually they become docile."

"What did you invent it for?"

"Originally, I was trying to make something that would help ease the emotional problems that happen after battles and other horrible experiences."

"PTSD," supplied Jordan.

"What?"

"We call that Post Traumatic Stress Disorder."

"That's a good name for it," Eohne chewed her lip. "Well, either way, it turned out to be far too powerful for that. It seemed to take away all memory and personality—not to mention language, social skills and powers of deduction and reason."

The ground began to rise and Jordan soon found herself panting from the effort of the climb. "So gnashwit basically makes them into a vegetable."

"Not quite. They do what they're told and they only have to be told once. When they get inducted, they're instructed on how to harvest the fungus and what kind of a schedule to work on and away they go. Never to deviate from it for the rest of their lives."

"That's horrifying," said Jordan, taking deep breaths. "But I still don't know if it's worse than execution or not."

"I know," said Eohne, not yet out of breath. "Sohne likes it, though and what Sohne wants, Sohne gets."

"Couldn't you still invent a reversal?"

Eohne frowned. "I've tried and failed so many times, I can't even tell you. Sohne has got me working on other things now, so I haven't had time." They crested a hill and a glade opened up before them. "Here we are." The women stopped at the edge of the clearing. Jordan took several deep breaths to calm her heart.

The glade was unremarkable, just a wide oval of grasses and wildflowers at the crest of a hill. After a moment's rest, they continued to the very top. A few stars appeared in the dim evening sky, their patterns utterly foreign to Jordan. Eohne took off her bag and held out her hand for the one Jordan carried. Jordan handed it to her and the two jars clinked against one another.

Eohne reached into the bag and pulled out a little sack. She upended the sack into her hand and a small brown bean tumbled into her palm, no larger than a coffee bean. She handed it to Jordan. "When I say, you need to swallow this."

"What is it?"

"A donisi pill."

"What will happen to me when I take it?"

"Nothing. It just needs to know where you want to send your message. When you swallow it, I need you to say your father's full name and his date of birth; include the hour and minutes, if you know them. Don't say anything else, or you'll dirty the frequency."

"I have no idea what hour he was born."

"That's okay, it probably won't need it." Eohne took out what looked like a smooth stone cylinder and held it. "Okay, go ahead and swallow it." She held up a finger and gave Jordan a warning look. "Don't speak until I tell you and just answer what I ask you."

Jordan nodded and her belly gave a little squeeze of anxiety. She put the brown pill into her mouth, but before she could swallow it, it slid to the back of her throat and halfway down her esophagus. Jordan clamped a hand over her mouth and tried not to cough. Her eyes bulged and she stared at Eohne; she felt like she had a marble stuck in her craw. She reached out and grabbed Eohne by the arm, squeezing hard. Fear clutched at her heart. This couldn't be right, something was wrong.

"It's okay," Eohne said. "I know it's unpleasant. Focus on my eyes."

Jordan's teal eyes flew to Eone's black ones and she sucked in a breath through her nose.

"What's your father's full name?"

Jordan tried to say, *'Allan Declin Kacy,'* but the words vibrated in her voicebox and went no further; nothing came out of her mouth. The vibration buzzed in her neck and Jordan squeezed her eyes shut at the horrible feeling.

"It's almost over," said Eohne. "When was he born?"

Again Jordan tried to speak–*'October 11, 1965'*–but the words backed up in her vocal cords and travelled no further than the blockage in her throat. A wave of nausea swept over her and the pill slid up to her mouth. She spat it out and Eohne caught it in her hand. Jordan bent over coughing, her hand at her throat. "Ow," she rasped.

"I know. I'm sorry about that," said Eohne, popping the lid off the stone cylinder and dropping the pill inside.

"You could have warned me," Jordan croaked. "That was awful."

Eohne handed her the waterskin. "I find it's better if we just get it over with."

Jordan snatched the waterskin and glared at Eohne. She upended the bag and took long swallows of water. The feeling of having a marble lodged in her neck began to ease. "What do you do with the pill?"

Eohne held up the cylinder. "It goes in here to dissolve."

"What's in there?"

"Just water." Eohne shook the cylinder and handed it to Jordan. "Hang onto that for a second." She rifled in her bag and pulled out what looked like a homemade syringe: A long needle attached to a hollow glass beaker with a plunger inside, depressed and ready to draw a substance into the belly of it.

Jordan shivered at the sight. "I hope you know you're not bringing that thing anywhere near me."

Eohne laughed. "Don't worry, it's not for you." She took out the first jar of bugs and handed it to Jordan. "Take this. Give me the cylinder." Jordan switched items with her and watched as Eohne took the lid off the cylinder and stuck the needle inside. As she pulled the plunger upward, a glowing neon green liquid filled the beaker.

"I thought you said that was water," said Jordan.

"It is, but now it has your vocal vibrations in it. Unscrew the lid and hand me one bug at a time." Eohne finished drawing up the liquid and dropped the cylinder onto the grass at their feet. She held out a hand. When Jordan hesitated, she laughed. "They don't bite."

Bracing herself, Jordan unscrewed the lid and took out a glass ball. "Ugh," she shivered as the thing sprouted legs in her hand. She dropped it into Eohne's palm. Eohne inserted the needle into a pinhole in the belly of the bug and injected a small amount of the green liquid. The center of the bug turned green. Eohne lifted it into the air and let go. The bug hovered there, its legs crawling slowly. Jordan watched, fascinated, as Eohne repeated this with every bug, until there were two dozen green balls with legs hanging in the air just above their heads. Eohne put the cylinder and the syringe back in the bag and straightened.

"Do you know what you want to say?"

"Uh," Jordan froze. She hadn't actually thought about it. *What can I say to my father?* She asked a simpler question of Eohne. "How are these bugs going to deliver the message? I mean what does it look like?"

"They move together to make lines of light between them," the Elf answered. "You should think fast, because the frequency won't hold forever. Tell me when you're ready and speak clearly when I give you the signal."

"Ack! Um, okay..." Jordan closed her eyes. *Allan is going to freak out when these weird glass balls show up and make lights, but it's too late to turn back now.* She nodded to Eohne.

"*Archi*," said Eohne to the bugs; the word was sharp and loud. She gestured for Jordan to proceed.

Keeping things as simple as she could, Jordan dictated her message uneasily. She wasn't so sure this was a good idea anymore. *What if those things give my poor dad a heart attack?* She finished and nodded to Eohne that she was done.

"*Telos*," barked Eohne and the bugs shot up into the air and zipped off so fast Jordan hardly had time to register what was happening. She craned her neck in search of them, but they were completely gone from view.

"How will they find him?"

"They'll home in on your father's frequency and find the nearest portal. They'll ask him to confirm he is Allan Declin Kacy before delivering the message."

Jordan covered her mouth with her hand and her eyes widened as a flood of new questions came to her mind. *What if Allan isn't alone? What if the bugs find him when he's with somebody and he finds out about the portal in our backyard? Scientists and the press will be crawling all over our place; it'll be my father's worst nightmare. But then, what if he is alone and they scare him out of his wits?*

Jordan felt her armpits grow damp as the impact of what she'd done began to hit home.

"Are you okay?" Eohne asked, her brows drawing together with concern. She put a hand on Jordan's shoulder.

"Call them back," Jordan croaked. "This was a bad idea."

Eohne's brows shot up. "I can't! There is no reversing them once they've been given a message. Why? What's wrong?"

Jordan couldn't find the words to express the anxiety that had taken root in her gut. She closed her eyes and put a palm to her forehead. A wave of nausea passed through her. For better or worse, Allan would be getting a very freaky visit from an alternate universe.

CHAPTER 19

*I*n spite of her exhaustion, Jordan tossed and turned all night, wondering how long the bugs would take to find Allan, how he might react, what he might do. She comforted herself with the thought that at least he would know she hadn't been kidnapped or murdered–that she was alive and had intentions of getting home as soon as she found her mother; *or as soon as is reasonable, anyway.* Jordan had resisted the urge to explain through the messenger bugs and kept her words as simple as possible. Too much explaining would just lead to more questions and more worry for Allan. *Or maybe I should have explained more? Maybe such a simple message would leave too much room for doubt that the message was some kind of sick joke. Why didn't I add some secret code word or phrase, something only he and I know, that would prove it was me who sent the message?* she lamented.

Peace, Jordan. She took deep breaths and began to count sheep. She focused on the sound of chirping insects and other nocturnal creatures. She heard Eohne breathing heavily on the loft below her and worked to match her breathing to the Elf's.

Just as Jordan was beginning to drift off to sleep on a cot on the highest loft in Eohne's hut, a fresh wave of questions revived her. *When the messenger bugs get back, should I use them to send a message to my mother?* She could recall her exact birth year easily because it had been inscribed on the family mausoleum: June 19, 1967. *But what if I'm wrong about my mother and she is dead? What would the bugs do then? Hang in front of the mausoleum asking for Jaclyn Peyton Kacy until the groundskeeper comes along and has a heart attack?* Jordan flopped over onto her belly and sighed. But her mother was alive. She could feel it. She believed it with everything inside her. It was too weird, her mother disappearing while wearing the locket. *But then, how had Maria gotten the locket? My mother had to have come back to make that possible and if my mother did come back, she would have come home.* On and on it went, each thought chasing another on an endless merry-go-round of insomnia-fueled mania. Or was it the mania that fueled the insomnia?

* * *

"You didn't sleep," said Eohne from the doorway, as Jordan made her way slowly down the vine ladder the next morning.

"Did I keep you awake?" Jordan's jaw creaked with a yawn as her bare feet found the hard-packed dirt floor. Her blouse was untucked and hanging out like a wrinkled nightshirt. Her indigo vest was undone, the leather thongs dangling and her stockings were hung over her shoulder. Her hair stood up like it had been teased by a monkey.

"No. You just look like you were up all night." Eohne left the door open and crossed the small space. She had a handful of greenery in her hand. She pulled down a mortar and pestle and began to tear the tender leaves into the bowl. She eyed Jordan, watching her grind at her eyes with her fists. "I have something that will help."

Jordan gave a second jaw-cracking yawn as she dragged herself to the door where her boots, knives, sheath and the tattered remains of her cloak were piled on a chair. She began to put herself together, slowly, with eyes at half-mast. "Is it coffee? Please say you have coffee."

Eohne bruised the leaves with the pestle and put them into a ceramic cup. She added springwater from a jug and watched as the water turned green from the leaf juice. "Sohne likes coffee," said Eohne. "Brings it in from goodness knows where. I never acquired a taste for the stuff. Too bitter for me."

Jordan plopped down on her butt to lace up her boots. "Will she share?"

Eohne walked to Jordan with the ceramic cup and handed it to her. "You won't need any after you have this."

"What is it?" Jordan took the cup and sniffed. She wrinkled her nose. "Smells like wet dog." She handed it back to Eohne.

"Yallawort." Eohne pushed the cup back at Jordan. "Drink. All of it. You'll need it."

Jordan took a cautious sip and shuddered. "*Eurgh*. That's vile."

"Drink," Eohne insisted again.

Jordan plugged her nose and threw back the rest of the nasty stuff. Her cheeks ballooned out and she looked at Eohne as she struggled to swallow. With a final gulp, her body shuddered with disgust. "I hope you realize how much this means I trust you," said Jordan, handing the cup back and looking up at the doe-eyed Elf. "After yesterday, trusting you is a miracle," she added, remembering the awful choking sensation from the evening before. "That pill was nas—"

Jordan blinked as a warm feeling spread through her organs and out into each limb. She felt like a thirsty plant taking in water–her fronds were perking up, her lifeless droopy stems were straightening and reaching for the sun. Her eyes widened. "Wow." She flexed her hands and made fists. She felt like they were so strong they could crack nuts. "Can I get some of that dog-water to go, please?"

Eohne gave Jordan a knowing smile and took the cup back to her little lab kitchen. "Your friend is awake," she said.

Jordan's head snapped to the Elf's face, her brows up. "Sol is awake?" She scrambled to her feet. "How is he?" She crammed her blouse down into her leggings and began lacing up her vest. "Have you seen him? Has he made a deal with Sohne for his wings yet? Can I see him?" She yanked Sol's satchels over her head and pulled her frazzled hair out from underneath the straps. She jammed a hand through one wrist cuff and tried to do up the laces with one hand.

"Yes, you can see him." Eohne came over to Jordan. "Here, let me." She tightened the laces on Jordan's cuffs.

Jordan danced in place while Eohne finished up. She stepped into her sheath and shimmied it up over her hips as she headed out the door, tightening the straps and buckles at her hipbone.

Morning light beamed down through the canopy in shafts, illuminating the Charra-Rae network of pathways and organic wood constructions. The gnashwits were already at work in the treetops, harvesting fungus. Birds looped around in the canopy, filling the air with whistles and songs. Jordan barely noticed any of it as she made her way down through the hole in the earth and along the ledge to the pathway. Eohne followed mutely, watching as Jordan raked her fingers through her hair, trying to put it into some kind of order.

Jordan took the stone path to the clearing two steps at a time. On the bottom step, she looked up and halted. Her heart leapt into her throat. She didn't even feel Eohne come up and stop behind her. Sol was there.

He was standing outside the little hut he'd presumably spent the night in. He stood with his back to Jordan, speaking with Sohne. Jordan lost all power of movement and speech as her eyes took him in.

Enormous tawny wings with white, tan and brown markings arched high up over Sol's head. They were folded closed behind him and the bottom tips crossed each other just above Sol's ankles and curved outward to the side. If they had hung down straight, they would be dragging in the dirt. A shaft of sunlight illuminated his glossy feathers. Jordan realized in that moment that Sol was entirely different from Toth. She'd been expecting the same leathery wings as the mercenary, complete with the powerful hooked claw at the top joint. But Sol's wings were like eagle's wings, thickly feathered and with a single joint.

Sohne's eyes found Jordan's over Sol's shoulder and she said something to Sol. Sol turned his head and saw Jordan staring at him. His face broke into a grin and he turned fully into the clearing to face her.

Jordan stood rooted to the spot, her mouth dry as she took in her friend in his true form.

It took Sol a second to remember that Jordan was from Earth. She'd seen a Nycht, but she'd never seen an Arpak before. It explained why her eyes were so big right now.

Slowly, Sol spread his wings out wide, opening them out so she could see them.

Jordan's breath caught in her throat as Sol's beautiful tawny wings stretched outward for so long she thought they'd never stop. The insides of his wings were a light tan color at the edges, fading to white. Jordan's eyes took in the scope of them, the tips of his outermost feathers reaching outward and up toward the canopy. Each wing was at least twice as long as Sol was tall, making his wingspan well over twenty-five feet. Jordan guessed it might be closer to thirty.

Sol waved his wings gently, the feathers swaying back and forth as if beckoning Jordan to come to him. In that moment, she suspected that every artist who had ever rendered an angel must have seen an Arpak, for that was exactly what he looked like—a rugged, powerful angel.

Sol's color had returned and he looked as though he'd never been injured, let alone on the edge of death. Sol folded his wings down again and watched Jordan approach. Her hair was bushy and stuck up in every direction, her vest had the laces done up in the wrong holes so that it sat crooked and bits of blouse bulged out at her waist. Her boots gaped around her calves, not yet done up and the laces of her blouse dangled down her chest, untied. He noticed she wore his satchels and that they were too big on her, dangling halfway down her thighs. Though there were dark smudges under her eyes, they were bright and her cheeks were flushed as she stopped in front of him. *I've never seen anyone look more beautiful.* He bit off the thought before it could go any further.

Jordan watched Sol's expression flash from happiness to something like admiration–then a gate slammed down and his expression went carefully blank. A confusion of emotion crashed through her as she watched his expression flicker from one to another as quickly as a fish flashing at the surface of a pond. Brushing all that aside, she threw her arms around his neck and squeezed him tight.

Sol gave a surprised laugh and hugged her back.

"You're okay," said Jordan into his neck, his hair tickling her lips. She squeezed him hard, feeling the solidness of him, his warmth, the life and health coursing through him. She pulled back. "You're magnificent," she said, her face alight, her gaze flicking over his tawny wings and back to his face.

Sol's face flushed red as he let her go. "I don't know about 'magnificent,' but I'm alive. Thanks to you," he said. He fought the urge to cross his arms over his chest to protect himself. The expression on Jordan's face skewered his heart like a kebab. He scrambled to stonewall against her authentic joy, her appeal. He swallowed hard, his mouth suddenly dry. He needed to get away from this human woman. He began to calculate in his head how quickly Sohne might be able to get Jordan back through a portal to Virginia, where she belonged.

"Did it cost you a lot?" Jordan asked, keeping her voice low and flicking her eyes to Sohne, where she stood a ways behind them, watching. Jordan took Sol's two satchels off her body and handed them back to him.

"She took gold," Sol said, surprised. "Unusual for an Elf, but I'm glad." He shrugged and smiled.

"I'm afraid it won't be quite that easy for you," came Sohne's voice.

Jordan and Sol turned to face the redheaded Elf. Jordan felt that voice twang at her nerves again, playing them like a violin.

Sohne's eyes were on Jordan and her arms were crossed like she meant business. Her long, tapered fingers splayed over her forearm like a resting spider.

"What do you want in exchange for helping me to find my mother?" Jordan asked, bracing herself. She really had nothing to give but her labor. There was no way she would give up her locket.

But Sohne's elegant brows arched and her eyes widened with surprise. Her lips parted and she uncrossed her arms. "Your mother?"

"Yes." Jordan began to pull the locket out from under her blouse.

"You don't want your wings back, too?"

Jordan laughed. "Wings?" Her gaze flicked uneasily between Sohne and Sol and back again. "I'm no Strix. I'm just looking for my mother; Jaclyn. I'm fairly certain she's somewhere here in Oriceran." Jordan stopped talking when she felt Eohne step up behind her.

"She doesn't know," said Eohne to Sohne. Jordan thought the dark-eyed Elf looked very serious.

"Know what?"

"Yes, 'know what'?" Sol's voice was hard.

Eohne and Sohne shared a look. Eohne's lips parted and Sohne shook her head; the movement was almost imperceptible. Sohne held a hand out to Jordan. "Walk with me."

Sol opened his mouth to protest, but Sohne held her palm up, cutting him off.

Jordan fell in step beside Sohne. They moved away from Sol and Eohne, though Jordan could feel their eyes on her back.

Sohne's shoulder brushed Jordan's. "Where are you from, Jordan? Answer truthfully."

Jordan felt Sohne's voice vibrate inside her; somehow stronger than before, even though the Elf had spoken quietly. "Richmond, Virginia," said Jordan.

"You were born there? On Earth?"

Jordan nodded.

"The ones who raised you, they are human?"

"Of course!"

Sohne's hand hooked the inside of Jordan's elbow. Her touch was gentle, soothing even. "My dear, you are an Arpak descendant."

The words rang through Jordan, echoing and repeating on a loop, searching for somewhere to purchase. She shook her head. "That's impossible."

Sohne's expression was as serious as Eohne's had been. "I don't know what you've been through, or why your parents never told you; I suppose it's possible they don't know. But somewhere in your bloodline, there is Arpak. I am certain."

Jordan's pulse quickened. "How do you know?"

"All species have a frequency. The elves of Charra-Rae are masters of frequency. It's what all of our magic is based on." Sohne lowered her chin to emphasize her next words. "You vibrate like an Arpak." She nodded toward Sol. "Even stronger than he does."

Jordan's eyes found Sol. He was staring at the two of them, eyes narrowed. She turned back to Sohne. "My mother—" she began.

"Was she Arpak?"

"I didn't think so, but..." Things were starting to piece themselves together. Jaclyn had to be from Oriceran. "Can I have a minute?"

"Of course." Sohne stepped back. "Take all the time you need."

"Thanks." Jordan walked away from Sohne, away from Sol and Eohne, down a narrow path toward the river. She crouched on a rock and splashed cold water onto her face. She covered her eyes with her fingers, blocking out the foreign world of Charra-Rae. *Could it be true? Jaclyn was an Arpak? Originally from Oriceran? Not an Earthling. Not even human.* Jordan had been right, her mother was somewhere in Oriceran, but she was wrong about one critical fact. Jaclyn hadn't fallen accidentally through the portal in their backyard. Jaclyn had come back intentionally. If Sohne was right, Jaclyn had simply gone home.

CHAPTER 20

"What's going on?" Sol demanded as Sohne returned to where he and Eohne were standing. "What did you tell her?"

"Only the truth," said Sohne. "She's Arpak."

Sol took a step back as though he'd taken a blow. "That's not possible." He ground the words out, like he was crushing a hard nut between his molars.

"It is," replied Sohne.

Sol itched to put his hands around the Elf's neck. He flexed his hands at his sides. "Why are you telling her lies?" He pointed to where Jordan was crouched at the river with her back to them. Goodness knew what torment she was going through right now. "That woman is human. She had no idea that Oriceran even existed when I met her. She needs to go back home to her family, not—"

"She's an Arpak descendant, Sol," replied Sohne. "I don't know how it happened, but it's true."

Sol gave her a dangerous look. "I don't know what kind of sick joke this is, but if you give a human girl Arpak wings—"

Sohne's sparkling laugh cut off his words, twanging through

his insides. "I can't do that, Sol. All I can do is bring out what is already there. If it wasn't already written into her genetic code, I couldn't put it there just because I wanted to." She chuckled again, crossing her long pale arms. "Really, you flatter me."

Sol's eyes flashed to Jordan's back as she stood up. He watched her rake her hair back from her face and pull it into a side braid. Her movements were calm, methodical. She looked so at peace from the back that Sol feared she might have become unhinged. He opened his mouth to threaten Sohne again, but Jordan turned and began walking toward them. Her face was unreadable. He watched her approach and felt his heart thud with dread at every step she took. Jordan's teal eyes were glacial. *I'd give the mysterious letter in my satchel to know what she's thinking right now.* The treasonous thought was so unlike him that he shuddered.

The two Elves and the Arpak watched Jordan approach, finishing her braid. She looked at Sol first. "It explains my eyesight." Her voice was clear and strong.

Sol blinked, taking a minute to work out what she meant. It felt like it was years ago that she had first asked him why her eyesight would be so much better on Oriceran.

Jordan looked at the elven women. "My eyes were dreadful on Earth. I was blind as a bat without my glasses or contacts. As soon as I came through to Oriceran, they cleared up." She snapped her fingers. "Just like that." Her eyes found Sol's again. "Now I know why."

There was something in Jordan's voice that gave Sol a chill. It had an edge that he'd never heard there before. Jordan was pissed. No, not just pissed. Livid. Sol felt his world tilt on its axis and all his plans for getting Jordan home as quickly as possible slid and fell off, tumbling into blackness.

Jordan levelled Sohne with a calculating look. Her jaw was set. "What do you want?"

"Jordan—" Sol began.

Jordan ignored him. "My wings. What do you want for them?"

She placed her hands on her hips. "I don't have gold. And don't think you're going to gnashwit my brains." She pointed at the Elf and shook her finger. "You can forget that idea right now."

Sohne gave a delighted laugh. "My dear, why would I ever want to do that to you? You're no criminal." She raised an eyebrow. "Are you?"

"Of course not," Jordan spluttered.

"Gnashwit?" Sol echoed.

"So? What do you want? Months of servitude?" Jordan went on.

The hair stood up on Sol's arms at the determination in Jordan's voice. He had no doubt she would give Sohne whatever she asked for and the thought terrified him.

"Just a promise," Sohne said. "That's all I want."

"Oh no," Sol put a hand over his forehead. "Jordan, don't do it. No matter what she wants, don't promise it. It's a bad idea."

Sohne raised her brows innocently at the Arpak. "Why would you say that?"

"What promise?" Jordan crossed her arms.

"I want you to promise that the next time you lose your wings, you'll come and see me. You won't go to any other Elves for help."

"Next time..." Jordan trailed off, confused. "There will be a next time?"

"I believe there will be," said Sohne.

They all waited for more information, but Sohne gave none. She was cryptic to a fault.

"Think about it, Jordan," Sol said. "You'll never see your dad again; not without losing your wings to do it. She knows you'll want to go back to Earth at some point. Probably soon."

Jordan chewed her lip. *It doesn't seem so bad. The promise is uncomplicated and seems to be in my interest.*

"Done," Jordan said. "I promise that the next time I lose my wings, I'll come and see you. I won't go to any other Elves." She held out her hand.

A slow, glittering smile spread across Sohne's face as she took Jordan's hand and shook it. "Good. Then come with me and let's see about those wings."

Sol and Eohne watched them go. Eohne looked at the Arpak in front of her, the one with his eyes on Jordan's back. A line had formed between his brows. "You don't look happy," said Eohne. "Don't you want to see her inherit her true form?"

"It's not that," said Sol, his mouth set in a grim line. "It's just that I know what comes next."

* * *

"I BELIEVE there is a theory in your world," said Sohne as they walked through the grove to the same hut where Sol had lain near death. "For every action, there is an equal and opposite reaction."

"Yes," said Jordan, cautiously. *Where is she going with this?*

"Our magic has a similar law."

"I'm not sure I'm following."

They stopped at Sohne's healing hut and the Elf ducked inside. "Be back in a moment," came her voice from inside the hut. When she reappeared, she had a small fabric bag over her shoulder. "This way," Sohne said, leading Jordan to a narrow trail through the ferns.

"Where are we going?"

"Away from Sol."

"Why?"

"I don't want to be anywhere near him when the screaming starts."

Jordan stumbled and righted herself. "Screaming?"

"Like I was saying, our magic comes with a price."

"Then how is it magic?" Jordan cried, her skin growing clammy at the thought of the kind of pain that warranted screaming. "Isn't the very definition of magic the ability to make something happen that counters the laws of physics? No consequences?" She caught up to Sohne, the ferns whipping against her legs. The earth was soft and moist and covered in mulchy leaves and needles; their footsteps were silent. "You know, snap your fingers and make a cake, or throw some pink dust and conjure up a pair of wings."

"It's not that simple," replied Sohne. The trail widened and Jordan fell into step beside the Elf. "Some magic might be that way, but ours isn't."

"Right. It's based on frequency. You and Eohne both mentioned that, but what does that mean for me?"

Sohne shot Jordan a look. "It means we can give you your wings, but only by manifesting a dormant gene in your DNA. You already have the ability to grow wings." Sohne put out an arm to brush aside a cluster of vines. "We're going to force your body to do that at a much faster rate than it would by itself."

Jordan felt ice-chips fill her gut. "That sounds agonizing."

"It is," replied Sohne.

"How agonizing?"

"Unbearable, from what I understand. But that's why I brought this," she patted the bag on her shoulder.

"What's in there? A painkiller?"

"Of sorts." Sohne led Jordan across a small bridge that arched over a trickling stream and the two hiked uphill. "The best thing you can do to prepare is to oxygenate your body. So for the rest of our little walk, I want you to take deep breaths."

"No problem there," said Jordan, beginning to pant as the climb got steeper. The two hiked on for another twenty minutes, with Jordan focusing only on her breathing.

When they came to a clearing where the canopy was high above their heads and the same clear stream was nearby, Sohne stopped. "Here we are." She took the bag off her shoulder and took out a tiny article of clothing. "Best put this on."

Jordan took the article and held it up. "It's…a bra. Sort of." It was only a single piece of fabric, without any straps to hold it on. "How is this useful?"

"It'll stay when you put it on. We need your shoulder blades uncovered."

"Right." Jordan turned her back to Sohne and wormed out of her vest and blouse. She laid them on a nearby log and held up the bra. It was the strangest material she'd ever seen. Though it wasn't on a body yet, it managed somehow to hold itself in shape as though it was. Jordan put it over her breasts and the material seemed to grab them–holding itself in place. "Cool," she looked down, admiring the shape it gave her. "Can we include this in our trade? It's genius." She turned to face Sohne.

The Elf smiled. "It's yours. It's one of Eohne's more elegant inventions."

Next, Sohne removed from the bag a small clear jar with a cork in it. The bottle hidden in the Elf's palm, Jordan couldn't see what was inside. She pulled out a second bottle, a wide-mouthed one with no lid. She handed it to Jordan. "I need you to make water in this."

"'Make water?'" Jordan wrinkled her nose. "Oh, pee." She took the jar, found privacy in the shrubs and urinated into the container. She set the jar on a stone while she put her leggings and holster back in place and then made her way back to Sohne, trying not to spill. "Here you go. A present, from me to you. Don't spend it all in one place."

Sohne cocked an eyebrow. "A joker. How quaint."

"What are you going to do with it?"

"Your frequency is in this liquid," said Sohne. "I'm going to use it to tap into the frequency of the rest of the water in your body. But I need you to put this guy against your skin first." Sohne handed her the other jar and Jordan took it, peering through the glass.

"Holy Hannah, what is that?" Jordan almost dropped the jar. She made a face at the nasty looking insect inside. It was black with purple stripes; or purple with black stripes, Jordan wasn't sure. Either way, it looked like a psychedelic hornet. It was twice the size of a normal hornet, with a long, vicious stinger. Jordan held the jar up and peered in at the critter again. "Is this really necessary?"

"Only if you want to dull the pain," said Sohne. She had retrieved a small ceramic platter the size of a dessert plate and she held it in her palm. She poured Jordan's pee onto the plate. "Hurry, please. Your frequency will begin to break down."

"Dammit!" Jordan danced from foot to foot. She took a breath and grabbed the cork. Her eyes met Sohne's. "I kind of hate you right now." She yanked out the cork and pressed the mouth of the jar to her forearm. She winced and squeezed her eyes shut. She jumped at the sting, but it wasn't nearly as painful as she'd anticipated. "That wasn't so baaaaaaaaa—"

Her legs wobbled and then melted into goo. Her vision turned into a swirly blur of color and she hit the forest floor. Her tongue felt larger than her head and her whole body turned to jelly. She could no longer make out Sohne's shape. The Elf was just a long alien figure, with long arms and fingers, that was fuzzy around the edges. Jordan tried to speak, but what emerged was a sloppy drone of random syllables. The shape that used to be an Elf murmured something, but all Jordan could hear was a buzz in her ears. When the pain came, it was blunt and aimless, wandering throughout her torso and back like a heavy roller made of hard rubber. Noise came from everywhere; long drones and short buzzes and a few higher pitched wavering notes. Jordan didn't have the ability to string rational thought together any longer. She had transformed into nothing but dull pain and alien sensations.

* * *

THE WORLD WAS full of sideways trees. Jordan inhaled with a start and a dull ache in her back and shoulders made her groan. Her first movement was to wipe moisture from her cheek from where she had drooled into the forest floor. She smacked herself in the face with floppy fingers. "Shohn," she croaked.

"Drink this," came the Elf's voice. A jar of clear liquid appeared in front of her face. "Slowly."

"Peed in 'at," mumbled Jordan.

"I washed it."

Jordan took more than a few moments to curl her fingers around the small jar and get her shoulder to take the weight of her arm and the cup. It took another several moments to lift her head. The world spun and Jordan froze and closed her eyes until it passed. She took a breath, opened her eyes and guided the cup slowly to her lips, taking the slowest, most laborious swallows she'd ever taken in her life. Sohne took the cup from her. Jordan's head was still really close to the ground. She tried to push herself up to sitting, but it felt like there was a weight holding her down. "Whash'appen ng?"

"You've never had wings before," said Sohne. "Your body has to get used to them. Your musculature needs time to develop." Sohne's foot appeared beside Jordan's head and then her hand appeared. "Take my hand. Just concentrate on getting up. One thing at a time."

Jordan took the Elf's hand and braced herself on the support Sohne offered. Jordan turned her head. The arch of a pale yellow feathered wing was just visible in her periphery. She pulled herself up to sitting and that's when the actual sensation of having wings hit her. "Oh," she said, her eyes going wide. It was like having another set of arms; long, slender arms, covered in feathers, that folded in an entirely different way than her human arms.

Sohne took much of Jordan's weight as she pulled the woman to her feet. Jordan staggered, her heart pounding with the effort. Wings appeared in both sides of her peripheral vision. "Oh, my…"

She looked up and back. The insides of her wings were white and soft. The tips of the outermost feathers were yellow. She opened them out and in, flexing them for the first time. They were enormous and stretched out far and wide on either side of her, just like Sol's did. The new joints in her back creaked as she flexed them for the first time. The weight of her wings pulled down on her collarbones and scapula, stretching the muscles on the sides of her neck in a new way. The movement radiated through her back and out into each shoulder. She rotated the wings forward, perpendicular to her spine. The tops of her wings were soft yellow and as they tilted further forward, she saw the outsides of them.

She gasped. "I'm a freaking canary!"

The outsides of her wings were a bright yellow. The color wasn't pure, as the larger feathers towards the outsides of her wings faded to brown. She groaned anyway. "Yellow? Really?" She glared at Sohne. "I hate yellow."

Sohne covered her mouth with a hand and Jordan was sure the Elf was trying not to laugh. "I have nothing to do with the color," she said. She held out a palm, "You are blonde, after all." She cocked her head. "They're beautiful."

"*Ugggghhhh*," Jordan groaned. And then the realization that she had wings really sank in and a grin crossed her face. "Where's Sol? I need to learn how to use these things."

CHAPTER 21

"She'll be okay," said Eohne, watching Sol pace like a caged animal. He hadn't stopped circling the clearing since Sohne and Jordan had disappeared.

Sol gave her a tight-lipped smile and nodded. *I should be on my way to Maticaw by now. I am incredibly late with my delivery.* And yet it wasn't his professional problems that were making him wear a path into the dirt. It was so many other things and all of them had something to do with the human woman who wasn't actually *human*. It had been hard enough keeping his distance knowing she had to go back to Earth; what did it mean now that she was rightfully a citizen of Oriceran? What kinds of barriers could he throw up between them now?

His face brightened when the bush beyond the hut rustled and he made out the tops of a set of pale yellow wings. When Sohne emerged from the bush, Sol almost put his neck out trying to see around her. And when the rest of Jordan came into view, his heart tripped on its wheel and his breath caught. Jordan's eyes met his and she smiled.

Sol's wings vibrated, a small and sudden flutter. The movement was involuntary; Jordan's eyes caught it and her wings mimicked his, like their wings were greeting one another. His eyes skimmed her torso and his face heated. She was wearing only a slip of fabric, twisted in the middle and winging out to cover her breasts. Her stomach and chest were pale next to the tanned skin of her shoulders and arms. As though remembering her near-nudity, Jordan crossed her arms.

"Sohne is having someone cut laces into the back of my vest," Jordan explained, blushing.

"Good idea," said Sol, whose face was also pink.

"You going to teach me what to do with these?" Jordan stretched her wings out.

He walked around her and took a look at the tops of her wings. His brows shot up at the bright yellow secondary feathers and the brown primary feathers. The scapular feathers in the center looked downy soft and light yellow. "How tropical," Sol remarked, with the biggest grin he'd had in a long time.

She narrowed her eyes at Sol. "What's so funny?"

"Nothing," Sol wiped the goofy grin from his face. "Let's get you airborne."

* * *

"Ride the updraft," Sol yelled down at Jordan, who was flapping and juddering in the air like an aimless kite.

"How? *Ack*!" Jordan's heart jounced in her chest as she dropped and her stomach flew upward into her mouth.

"Let your legs trail behind you instead of hanging straight down, then open wide and just glide." Sol did a spiral and turned over to show her what he meant. He picked up speed and had to make a big loop before coming back to her.

"Showoff," Jordan muttered. "What if I fall out of the sky?" But Sol was out of range. "Good, now I'm talking to myself." She looked down at the hilltop below her, the same open glade where she and Eohne had sent the message to Allan. So far, she'd been too scared to go more than a dozen feet above the trees.

"Climb, Jordan," Sol yelled as he circled above her. "Don't hang out where it's the hardest to fly – there's nothing down there to climb with."

Jordan gave a few powerful flaps and began to climb laboriously. She grunted as she inched her way upward. "What are you grinning at now?" she asked when she caught Sol's expression.

"You know your wings can operate separately from your arms, right?" He said, dimpling on both sides of his mouth.

"Oh, right." Jordan stopped flapping her arms and let her wings move independently. She caught an updraft and her wings opened out, feeling stretched. "Whoa," she cried as she flew upward. "Sol!" She squealed, feeling like a leaf in a tornado.

"Stop thinking so hard," Sol called. "Your wings are made for this. Let them do the work. It's like walking. Do you think about your legs moving when you walk?"

Jordan didn't answer, her heart was pounding too hard. She closed her eyes as a wave of dizziness washed over her. But as her vision blanked out, something wonderful happened: her wings grabbed the air and propelled her upward and forward. Jordan gasped at the sensation. Her eyes flew open, but her wings and body held steady. The powerful flaps took the energy swirling around her, found the currents and righted her. "Sol, I'm doing it!" She laughed, breathlessly.

"Nice work." Sol's voice came from above her. She looked up. Sol flew in an arch over her, passing her while upside down.

"How is that even possible?" Jordan's wings gave an ache as adrenalin flooded them.

"I've been flying for a while, now," said Sol, barrel rolling to hover in front of her, his chest facing hers. "Like anything else, it's just a matter of putting the hours in. By the time we get to Maticaw, you'll be flying like a pro."

"Maticaw?"

"I have to make my delivery there," said Sol. "Then we can go on to Rodania."

Jordan's heart felt unexpectedly full. Sol was going to take her with him, not abandon her to fend for herself. Her wings burned and her heart pounded. Breathlessly she said, "I thought I was fit. I have to go down." She looked down at the canopy. "How do I get down?"

Landing and taking off were the most difficult parts of flying and Jordan was already struggling. "Let me help you with the first time," Sol said. Sol circled Jordan until he was directly behind her, matching her stroke for stroke. The wind from her wings blew his hair up and back from his face. He put his hands on her waist and steered her, flying them in tandem back to the glade. "Legs forward, wings out," Sol said, pulling her up and back, feet to the earth. They landed and Jordan took a few running steps as Sol let her go. "You'll get stronger quickly," said Sol. "You've just never used them before."

Jordan turned to face him, her eyes bright and face flushed. "That was amazing." She wanted to take off again, but her wings felt like they were made of sod. She folded them and let them relax. They throbbed with the effort the flight had taken.

"My mother has to be Arpak," Jordan said. "How else would this be possible?" Jordan could barely face the emotions that had come along with this revelation.

How had Jaclyn ended up on Earth? Why had she married a human? Why had she left her baby? Why hadn't she ever told Allan anything about what she was and where she was from? Why had she disappeared twice? Where was she now? What was she doing?

Jordan tried not to let the anger overtake her; there would be time for that later. She needed more answers; she needed to understand. There was a headstone back in Virginia for a beloved wife and mother who wasn't actually dead. There had better be a damn good reason for the deception.

Sol regarded her, his eyes now serious. "If she's an Arpak and she's here on Oriceran, then she's most likely in Rodania. That's your best bet for finding her. It's our capital."

Jordan nodded and her stomach gave a twist. She was closer than ever to unraveling the mystery of her mother's disappearance. "You'll take me there?"

"As long as you don't mind stopping off in Maticaw first," Sol said. "I have to complete this delivery, then we can go on to Rodania."

"How many days?"

"That depends on you," Sol nodded at her wings. "Whatever you can handle. Maticaw and Rodania are less than a day's journey apart.

"And how far is Maticaw?"

"If we leave tonight, we can be there by tomorrow evening." He gave her a look. "The first couple of days will be hard. You'll be sore. Are you ready for that?"

"What's a little soreness compared to what we've already been through? I'll be damned if I sit around here in Charra-Rae, doing flying exercises while my mother is so close." Her eyes found his and Sol found himself standing up straighter at the determination he saw there. "Let's get my things and go. Now. Today."

"As you wish," agreed Sol.

CHAPTER 22

The Kacy Estate

ALLAN HAD NEARLY WORN a trail into the wood of the front porch with his pacing. Jordan had been missing for over two weeks now. The evidence left behind was miniscule and yet massively disturbing in nature. A few droplets of blood connecting her favorite oak tree with the parlor, a bag of melted ice soaking the carpet and crushed patches of grass below the limbs of the oak were the only clues left behind.

Allan had almost fainted when he'd seen the first drop of blood drying on the wood of their back deck, but a righteous fury had brought him back around. Whoever had hurt his darling daughter was going to pay. The inspectors had combed every inch of the manor and the property like the bloodhounds they were. But state senator or not, Allan wouldn't hesitate to take things into his own hands. The law had failed miserably with Jaclyn—turning up no leads in over three years of investigation. Allan hoped they didn't fail with Jordan, too. At least they had more to go on: blood. Not much, but then, Allan didn't like *any* of his daughter's blood to be outside of her body.

No, sir. Not acceptable. Somebody is going to pay.

The pitying looks from the investigators could hardly be borne. Poor Allan Kacy. His wife vanished and two decades later, his daughter has vanished, too.

A few of the looks were laced with suspicion, but Allan had watertight alibis in both circumstances. The questions were endless. *Who are your enemies?* (Not 'Do you have enemies', for it was assumed that as a politician, they came with the territory.) *Did Jordan have any enemies that you know of? Do you know the passwords for Jordan's phone and laptop? Did she keep a journal? We'll need access to her diary and emails.*

Allan began to have nightmares and soon he was afraid to go to sleep. *My baby's blood has been spilled.* But the day Inspector Cranston pulled up in front of the manor, with the deep line between his eyes and news he was extremely hesitant to share, was the day Allan's world shifted on its axis.

"It's not Jordan's blood," Inspector Cranston said, standing on Allan's front porch.

Allan found himself unable to blink for a space of time that could have been ten seconds or a year; then relief flooded his limbs. He sank onto the wicker loveseat behind him. "It's not Jordan's blood," he echoed.

The inspector shook his head and pushed his glasses up his nose. He took a breath, as though to say something else, but then paused.

"Whose blood is it, then?"

Cranston put his hands into the pockets of his suit jacket. "We don't know that. I can tell you that it's from a male. It sheds a lot of light on the case, but only gives us the ability to match it to a suspect," he paused. "Or another victim."

Allan's eyes flashed to Cranston's face. "Another victim?" He thought this through. "I hope you're not insinuating that my daughter was the perpetrator, here. She's the one who's missing and she would never go anywhere without telling me first. She knows what it would do to me." He jabbed a finger toward the inspector. "My daughter is in trouble."

"We're not insinuating anything," the inspector said, his voice mild. "But it is not Jordan's blood that we took from your couch and your carpet and your lawn and your kitchen floor." He stopped there, his eyes dropped to the ground, frown lines deepening.

"What else?" Allan prompted. "Is there something else? Don't spare me just because she's my daughter. What else did you find?"

Cranston's mouth opened and then closed. "Nothing," he shook his head. "I'll be sure to call you immediately, as soon as the case unfolds. In the meantime, if you think of anything else that can help, even if it seems unimportant, you know how to reach me."

Allan nodded. He watched the inspector return to the car parked in the driveway.

Inspector Cranston's partner, Stevenson sat in the passenger side with a cell phone glued to his ear. Cranston opened the car door and slid into the driver's seat. Stevenson said goodbye and hung up.

"How did he take it?" Stevenson asked.

Cranston turned on the car, shifted it into drive and steered it around the rotunda, nodding to Allan through the glass as they pulled away. "I didn't tell him", Cranston said.

Stevenson stared at his partner. "Why not?"

"Because, it makes us look incompetent. I still think it's a mistake." He gripped the wheel until his knuckles whitened. "Peters made a mistake."

Stevenson dropped his chin and shot Cranston a hard look. "Peters never makes mistakes. Forty-four years in the lab makes him the best we've got. He's certainly not going to mess up blood-type–that's kindergarten stuff."

"I know, but…" Cranston clenched his jaw. "What am I supposed to say?"

"You have to tell him. Withholding it from him will only hurt us. He might know something about one of Jordan's friends." Stevenson waited for Cranston to slow the car. He didn't. "Phil," he prompted.

With a heavy sigh, Phil Cranston hit the brakes.

Stevenson's cell phone rang again and he put it to his ear.

* * *

ALLAN HEARD the car slow at the end of the long driveway. Crowds of journalists and parked vehicles were waiting on the other side of the closed gate. Allan had hired private security to keep the press off his property. He couldn't stop the helicopters and drones that passed overhead, but they'd become less frequent now that the activity on the Kacy Estate had died down. He'd passed through the worst of the media storm. He hoped.

Allan watched the brake lights of the inspector's car flash. The vehicle turned around in the road and made its way back to the house.

Leaving the car to idle and his partner to chatter on his cell, Inspector Cranston got out and approached the front porch where Allan was still sitting.

Cranston pulled out a kerchief and mopped the sweat from his brow.

"Forget something?" Allan said, getting to his feet.

"There's something else you should know," Cranston said, shifting uncomfortably from one foot to the other. "About the blood."

"Okay." Allan waited, the knuckles of his right hand coming up to rest on his hip.

"It's chimera blood."

"Chimera—" Allan blinked and shook his head. He dropped

his hand from his hip. "What?" What rose to mind were the illustrations of mixed up animal species from fantasy books that Allan had enjoyed as a kid. A lion's head, an eagle's wings, a man's face.

Cranston put out a hand. "Not like the chimera from mythology. It's a medical term—genetic chimerism. It just means a single organism composed of cells from different zygotes. In this case, it's resulted in two different blood types within one body."

Allan raked a hand through his hair and his brow furrowed. "What are you saying?"

Too late to turn back now. Cranston took a breath and plunged forward. "Whoever was here with your daughter may have some distinguishing features that would identify them as chimeric. It's not often that chimerism is easy to spot; people can go their whole lives not knowing that they have it. Normally, chimerism is subtle, or even undetectable, like a set of twins carrying each other's blood. But in this case, the two blood types are so vastly different that we think whoever—or whatever—bled on your floor, may have some kind of obvious non-human feature. But, frankly—" Cranston spread his hands wide. "We're shocked that this chimera is even alive."

"Why? What were the two blood types?"

Cranston blinked rapidly but didn't hesitate. "Human and avian."

"Excuse me?" Allan laughed suddenly. "I thought you said 'avian.'"

"I did."

Allan stopped laughing. Goosebumps swept his forearms and the back of his neck. "So, what, that means we're looking for a guy with a beak or something?" *This is nuts, I don't believe it. They made a mistake at the lab. A stupid mistake.* Allan wondered if he should bring in a private investigator on the side. His confidence in the police had just taken a tumble.

"We don't know," said Cranston. "There may be nothing

visibly different about him at all. We've never seen this before. Our lab techs would have said this kind of chimera was impossible, but, well, here we are. Chimera blood is not the same thing as hybrid blood. Hybrids are the result of crossbreeding." Cranston shuddered. "That's not the case here. Thank God."

Allan sat back down. "This just keeps getting weirder and weirder."

Cranston nodded. "Does it bring anything to mind for you? Any of Jordan's friends that maybe seem—"

He found himself unable to go on.

Allan cocked an eyebrow. "What? Bird-like?" He barked a laugh. "That's ridiculous."

"I know." Cranston agreed with him. It was ridiculous. For the third time in as many hours, Cranston questioned their lab tech's results. But they'd been triple-checked. "We just thought you should know." He dismissed himself again and this time, the car disappeared down the driveway, through the gate and down the road.

Around the time Cranston and Stevenson returned to the precinct was when Allan started drinking.

CHAPTER 23

*H*and still gripping the empty brandy bottle perched on his knee, Allan swung morosely to and fro on the oak's swinging chair. His unseeing eyes were locked in a frozen stare. *Chimera blood.* Allan had read as much as he could about genetic chimerism and had even gone so far as to call a few of Jordan's friends to ask them about their blood. The conversations hadn't gone well. It probably hadn't helped that Allan was slurring his words.

The flashing of little green lights in his periphery made Allan look up into the oak's branches. He squinted, thinking that his eyes were playing tricks on him. But, no, the flashing lights continued. Just like fireflies, only with longer and brighter flashes. The twinkling was not in his imagination. The flashes blurred together and became a green neon line; the line spelled out words, which burned brightly and then slowly began to fade. Allan jerked to his feet, his neck creaking as he tilted his head.

Minyma 6422 Allan Declin Kacy archi.

Allan blinked and squeezed his eyes shut, then opened them again. The message was still there, but then faded to nothing. But there was something in the tree still. At the corners of each letter were little round balls. The balls began to glow and move again, making another neon line of words.

Are you Allan Declin Kacy Born 1965?

Allan gasped and a hand flew to his mouth. His heart pounded in his ears. Allan snatched his spectacles from his pocket and put them on his face. The neon message held steady. Allan's mouth opened, but only a choked sound came out. The message began to flash urgently.

Are you Allan Declin Kacy Born October 11 1965?

"Yes, yes, that's me," Allan cried out.

I've gone crazy, he thought. *I've finally cracked. It's all been too much.*

The flashing neon sign seemed to hear him and began to fade away, satisfied. The little balls began to move again. There were probably two dozen of them and they dropped toward Allan, moving as one. They hung in the air under the branches of the oak, just above Allan's head. They began to move individually again, spelling out a new message without any punctuation.

Dad its me Jordan

Allan cried out and staggered backward, tripping and falling to his tailbone just the way his daughter had done only a mere week before. He scrambled to his feet, every hair standing upright.

"Jordan!" He yelled. "Jordan, can you hear me?!"

The words began to fade and Allan's heart beat even faster as the bugs spelled out the next words.

Im okay

"Oh, thank God," Allan closed his eyes for a brief moment. "Where are you?" He had no idea whether his daughter could hear him, but it was worth a shot. "Tell me where you are, Jordy!"

The last message faded and the balls spelled out a new one.

Dont be afraid

"Ha!" Allan loosed. "Too late for that." Allan staggered closer to the balls. Looking up at them, he realized they were so close he could almost reach out and grab one. He began to notice something else that was strange. Behind the glowing words was a backdrop that didn't make sense. Hazy clouds, moving across the limbs of the oak? Allan's eyes narrowed, trying to focus. The bugs began to move again, driving like little cars on rails. The words lit up between the balls.

I fell through a portal

Allan's face changed and he shook his head. "This is not possible," he whispered. But the words were there and the little balls spelling out the words were there. And that strange hazy background behind the words that looked nothing like the oak was there. And the balls were spelling more words.

I know it sounds crazy

Allan nodded, unconsciously agreeing with the message. But he found himself saying, "Jordy, sweetheart, are you trapped?"

The last message faded and the balls spelled the next line. No punctuation, no response to his question.

Ill come back soon

Allan's eyebrows shot up. *She'll come back soon. So she could come back. So why isn't she coming back right now?*

"When?" he asked the balls. The last message faded slowly. The balls moved again.

Minyma 6422 Allan Kacy télos

The blood drained from Allan's face. "No," he whispered and stepped closer to the balls, looking directly up at them. "When, Jordy? Whose blood is it, darling? Come back now!"

But there was no other message and the last one began to fade.

"No!" cried Allan.

Without thinking, he reached up and grabbed one of the balls, snatching it out of the air. His fist closed around something cool and hard and the size of a jumbo marble. He dropped it into his empty brandy bottle and jammed his thumb over the mouth.

These balls are my only connection to my only daughter.

Allan grabbed another and another. The lines of light between the balls disappeared abruptly as he snatched them out of the air and deposited them in his brandy bottle. *Clink. Clink. Clink.* One after the other. They were the only evidence that he wasn't as mad as the hatter. He wasn't able to get them all before the rest of the balls disappeared, swallowed up as though disappearing underwater. The last message was gone and the hazy scene dissipated like fog.

Allan stood there with his thumb jammed over the mouth of the bottle, his chest heaving. "Jordan?" he cried out, hoping for something more. Anything. He called her name several more times, but there was nothing. He yelled at the bottle full of balls. He held it up and peered through the glass. Pushing his specs up his nose and squinting at them, he was surprised to see how insectile they looked up close.

Most of the balls still looked like clear marbles with two small green lights inside. The little lights reminded him of eyes, since they were close together and positioned on one side. But it was the little ball that sprouted six clear little legs and began to climb up the inside of the bottle that made Allan take off running.

He raced inside the house with his thumb clamped over the bottle, to the sideboard where he'd left the cork. All the while, the little ball climbed towards Allan's thumb. He assumed it wouldn't bite, since he'd already touched them and they'd done nothing, but better safe than sorry. Plus he'd never really been a fan of insects–even if they were clear ones from an alternate universe.

Jamming the cork in place, Allan set the bottle on the sideboard and stepped back. He stood there for some time, watching as the other insects sprouted legs and began to crawl up the glass and on top of one another, looking for a way out.

FINIS

AUTHOR NOTES - A.L. KNORR

WRITTEN SEPTEMBER 3, 2017

Consuming stories is something I have loved since I was old enough to follow one, and telling stories has been my dream since about that same time. I used to stuff a towel in the crack under my bedroom door so my parents wouldn't tell me to close my book, turn off the light and go to bed. Books were my escape, my secret joy.

What I love about art is that the longer we do it for the better we get at it, but perfection is unattainable and that's a good thing. Because within the flaws lies the heart of what it means to be human. My goal as a storyteller is to connect with the reader in that heart, to give them a moment of insight that makes them nod their heads and say, "Yeah, and isn't that just how it is."

When I met Martha Carr, it took less than ten minutes to recognize that I'd found a kindred friend. I didn't know at the time the fortuitous relationship that would blossom from it, I just knew that hers was the kind of vibrant, enthusiastic, kind, relatable, and salt-of-the-earth spirit I wanted more of in my life.

When Martha called several months later to ask if I'd be interested in writing in an urban fantasy universe that she was developing with Michael Anderle (a man I have immense respect for), I didn't even hesitate to say yes.

I knew it would be work, I knew that starting another series before I was finished the one I was writing would be challenging. I knew that crossing over from elemental magic into stories with elves and trolls would stretch me as an artist. I knew that collaborative creation was unexplored terrain that could hold many potential obstacles. These are some of the reasons I said yes. How will I know what I can do if I don't stretch myself? It was a moment where I just held onto my proverbial hat and jumped in feet-first, hoping for the best.

We've barely gotten started building Oriceran and I am already so happy I said yes. From the moment we began to work together, a magic web has been weaving itself, knitting together and connecting the authors, the readers, and the publishing team. Isn't it amazing what can spring from visiting a world that only exists in our imagination? Is the joy, the laughter, the love, the triumph any less real than what we experience in our daily lives? I propose that it's *better* in some ways… but I'm biased.

I love a quote from Roy Williams of Wizard Academy, and I paraphrase:

"You have 100,000 times more synapses in your brain than sensory receptors in your body. Therefore, you are roughly 100,000 times better equipped to experience a world that *does not exist* than a world that does."

May lightning strike me the day that I forget that the reason I can do what I love is because of you, the reader. A hearty, authentic and joyful thank you to you for choosing to spend some of your reading time in our fantastical world. No, but for real, yo'. Thank you!

Thank you to the 'Just-in-time' team of proofreaders, and thank you to the publishing team at LMBPN. Thank you to my beta readers, my street team, my parents and brothers, and to my endlessly supportive circle of friends. I couldn't have done this without you.

AUTHOR NOTES - MARTHA CARR

WRITTEN SEPTEMBER 3, 2017

As a rule, I do my best to listen to that inner voice when it says to go and do something. It has always paid off in ways that have made people stand back and say, "How did you know?" I didn't know. I just felt it and went. I find out why, later.

One of those moments was when I noticed a post by Abby-Lynn Knorr in an author forum on Facebook. She was open, direct and full of useful information. (She had a kickass marketing spreadsheet and was willing to share) That started it all.

But it didn't take long before I noticed other things. Generosity, kindness and an optimism in life, in general. That inner voice said, 'she's going places that will be fun and full of magic. Make a note.'

Then, I watched her brand-new, first series ever that happened to be in urban fantasy – The Elemental Origins Series – take off. I wasn't surprised at all. I was happy and amazed. So cool when something unfolds and builds and brings so much fun to everyone involved. That voice said, 'See, I told you. But she's just beginning. This is only the seed of her literary wonderment.'

So, when Michael Anderle asked me to co-create an entire universe with him and that we would eventually add more authors, Abby-Lynn, who we call 'Abs', was at the top of my list. But Michael and I had also said that we would for sure, no doubt, we promise, not invite anyone else in till July. Give us a chance to figure things out first.

That lasted a few days. Michael called saying he had already told another author about what we were doing and could we start now? I said, sure but I have someone too.

Keep in mind, Abs (along with three other authors) agreed to go on this journey with us while it was still forming. We would get a question and then Michael and I would have to go have a chat to figure out the answer. Abs was on board with all of it. Not surprised. It was that optimistic, everything-will-be-full-of-wonder attitude that I noticed right away.

Here's the last thing I've noticed about everyone involved in this process – including Abby-Lynn Knorr. She never asked, 'what if' questions. You know, the ones where you picture the future (usually what you don't want) and ask, what do we do if that happens? I call those magical questions before there's no real answer to them. I can give you a positive answer as easily as a negative but the truth is, they're imaginary questions with imaginary answers. The past often doesn't even predict the future. The only honest answer possible is, I don't know. For a lot of people that's not enough and that's where you part ways.

But, when someone can go forward without having to ask those and believe that whatever happens we'll all figure it out because we believe in each other and what we're doing – magic happens. The real kind that changes lives.

Each of our new authors has displayed this trait and it has only enriched this new Universe till we are more of a family than anything else. Everyone is genuinely rooting for themselves and everyone else in this Oriceran family (By the way, pronounced Or-i-sar-en) and offers advice and encouragement along the way.

So, I'm going to pull a Babe Ruth here and point at the stands and say, 'Keep an eye out for what happens next. These authors are all going to do something amazing that will be fun and engaging and tell a good story.'

PUBLISHER NOTES - MICHAEL ANDERLE

WRITTEN SEPTEMBER 3, 2017

Wow, writing this will be an interesting challenge. Before I go too far, THANK YOU for not only reading this book, but also the Author, and now *Publisher*, notes at the back.

Most of you who know me, are used to reading my Author Notes and you might be scratching your head...

"Publisher Notes?"

Well, yes. It is because of the Kurtherian fans that I was able to consider creating a new universe with new ideas (or are we simply revealing the truth?)

A universe which is being built while the Kurtherian Gambit Universe is still undergoing major growth itself.

Eventually, I want to create a series in Oriceran with two characters that were the genesis of this new Universe for me. However, instead of creating a new series and universe from scratch, it will already have dozens of books and a rich history already ready for me to join in.

A universe with a vibrant community of authors, fans, stories, audio books, and artwork that will be ready for me to join.

However, those books come later. I'm still running LMBPN Publishing and responsible for two (2) series in the Kurtherian

Gambit Universe that need completion and another that needs to be started, or two.

Sigh, maybe next year I will get to that project – we shall see.

Anyway, this is my coming out note where for the first time in my career, I'm writing a note as the publisher.

I hope you like our work, and our efforts. If you have fun and/or enjoy the stories, please considering giving the authors a shout out on the Facebook page and let them know what you think.

While we certainly write to sell books, we creatives can't survive effectively on that only. We need *your* interactions to help keep us going emotionally.

Your funny, insightful and often poignant reviews help us every time we go back to the desk in our offices, or table at Starbucks, open our laptops or create a new Scrivener file and type.

"It was a dark and stormy night..."

Hopefully, as I grow my skills as a publisher, my company (LMBPN) will start to become something you search for on Amazon and Audible knowing there is a damned good chance we will have compelling stories for you to sink your imagination into, and just get away for a little while.

Ad Aeternitatem,
Michael Anderle

WANT MORE FROM ORICERAN

JOIN THE EMAIL LIST HERE:

http://oriceran.com/email/
Find the Oriceran Universe on Facebook:
https://www.facebook.com/OriceranUniverse/
Find the Oriceran Universe on Pinterest:
https://www.pinterest.com/lmbpn/pins/

The email list will be a way to share upcoming news and let you know about giveaways and other fun stuff. The Facebook group is a way for us to connect faster – in other words, a chat, plus a way to share new spy tools, ways to keep your information safe, and other cool information and stories. Plus, from time to time I'll share other great indie authors' upcoming worlds of magic and adventure. Signing up for the email list is an easy way to ensure you receive all of the big news and make sure you don't miss any major releases or updates.

Enjoy the new adventure!
    A.L. Knorr and Martha Carr 2017

A.L. KNORR SOCIAL

To be the first to learn about new releases and special offers, sign up for A.L. Knorr's newsletter here: https://www.alknorrbooks.com/

Facebook: https://www.facebook.com/alknorrbooks/
Instagram: https://www.instagram.com/alknorrbooks/?hl=en
Twitter: https://twitter.com/ALKnorrBooks
Pinterest: https://www.pinterest.com/ALKnorrBooks/

MARTHA CARR SOCIAL

Website and Email list: www.marthacarr.com

Facebook Page:
https://www.facebook.com/ChroniclesofLeira/

Facebook Fan Group:
https://www.facebook.com/groups/MarthaCarrFans/

OTHER BOOKS BY A.L. KNORR

Born of Water
(including novella The Wreck of Sybellen)
Born of Fire
Born of Earth
Born of Aether
Born of Air

The Kacy Chronicles

* with Martha Carr *
Descendant (1)
Ascendant (2)
Combatant (3)
Transcendent (4)

Other books and Stories

OTHER BOOKS BY A.L. KNORR

Pyro (including the novella Heat)
Returning Episode II

OTHER BOOKS BY MARTHA CARR

The Leira Chronicles
* with Michael Anderle *

[Waking Magic (1)](#)
Release of Magic (2)
Protection of Magic (3)
Rule of Magic (4)
Dealing in Magic (5)
Theft of Magic (6)
Enemies of Magic (7)
Guardians of Magic (8)

Rewriting Justice
(Leira 2.0)
* with Michael Anderle *
Justice Served Cold (Book 1 May 2018)

I Fear No Evil
* with Michael Anderle *
Kill the Willing (Book 1 May 2018)

OTHER BOOKS BY MARTHA CARR

School of Necessary Magic
* with Michael Anderle *
Dark is Her Nature (Book 1 May 2018)

The Soul Stone Mage Series
* with Sarah Noffke *

House of Enchanted (1)
The Dark Forest (2)
Mountain of Truth (3)
Land of Terran (4)
New Egypt (5)
Lancothy (6)
Virgo (7)

The Midwest Magic Chronicles
* with Flint Maxwell *

The Midwest Witch (1)
The Midwest Wanderer (2)
The Midwest Whisperer (3)
The Midwest War (4)

The Fairhaven Chronicles
* with S.M. Boyce *

Glow (1)
Shimmer (2)
Ember (3)
Nightfall (4)

Made in the USA
Las Vegas, NV
15 January 2022